TRU

GUARDIAN GROUP SECURITY TEAM BOOK 1

BREE LIVINGSTON

Edited by
CHRISTINA SCHRUNK

Bree Livingston Publishing LLC

Tru: Guardian Group Security Team Book 1

Copyright © 2021 by **Bree Livingston**

Edited by Christina Schrunk

https://www.facebook.com/christinaschrunk.editor

Proofread by Krista R. Burdine

https://www.facebook.com/iamgrammaresque

Cover design by Book Covers for $20

http://www.facebook.com/stunningcovers

Bree Livingston

https://www.breelivingston.com

Publisher's Note: This is a work of fiction. Names, characters, places, and incidents are a product of the author's imagination. Locales and public names are sometimes used for atmospheric purposes. Any resemblance to actual people, living or dead, or to businesses, companies, events, institutions, or locales is completely coincidental.

Tru: Guardian Group Security Team Book 1 / Bree Livingston. -- 1st ed.

ISBN: 9798712783922

To Nan,
I will always remember you holding your little black travel Bible and magnifying glass. That you loved hugging people. That you brought sunshine to people I love. You were a special lady. Go rest. I will make sure we meet again.

1

*T*ossing his duffle bag onto his shoulder, Thaddeus "Tru" Truman grabbed his shoes from the conveyer belt and finished his security check at JFK International Airport. He understood the need for the measures, but he hated the hassle, especially when he was one of the unlucky ones to be singled out and patted down. Oddly enough, he seemed to be unlucky a lot, which made flying a chore more often than not.

He hustled to the nearest gate, dropped his shoes to the floor, and sat on a bench as he sandwiched his phone between his shoulder and ear. This last-minute assignment was handed to him shortly before sunrise with only the name of the airport and time. It had worked out since his last case had wrapped up in New York City.

"Hey, security go okay?" asked Ryder, one of the resident computer experts at Guardian Group.

"If by okay you mean patted down, sure." Tru scanned the area out of habit before he slipped his shoes on, pausing when he spotted a young family walking by. With all of his siblings married, family was a sore spot for him. He wanted what they had, but his job made relationships difficult. Thoughts like those were for another time when he wasn't working.

Ryder laughed. "Sorry, man. I just sent you the file."

Finished with his shoes, Tru took the phone from his ear and checked his email. Kayleigh Kingston. Huh. Catchy name, cute photo. He put the phone back to his ear. "Is she a victim or target?" His gut said victim.

"Target."

Tru checked the file again, his brow wrinkling as he studied the woman's picture. Target? His gut was never wrong, but there was a first time for everything. "Okay."

"All the details are there. I've got her location pinged near a coffee shop roughly a quarter-mile from you, just as you reach the belly of the terminal. You'll need to be careful with this one. Don't let appearances fool you. She's ruthless."

Again, Tru looked at the photo and shook his head. What he was hearing and what he was gathering by instinct sat in complete opposition. "And we're sure?"

"Positive. We've got evidence that puts her at four murders. Three loose ends and a witness." Keyboard keys clacked. "The last left a two-year-old an orphan. Luckily, he has grandparents and they've agreed to take custody. There's a photo of him in her file."

A quick look at the little boy's picture had Tru rubbing the spot over his heart. That old ache from the loss of his baby brother would never get easier. Time healed all wounds, but the lack of justice just kept everything raw. His gut would have to take a back seat this time. "Are we working for the grandparents?"

"NYPD. London Carter is the mastermind behind a black-market art trade, and Kayleigh Kingston seems poised to take over the operation. The chief on the case, along with the detectives, reached out to us because they believe they have a mole on the team, and we agreed to help. We had to work quickly because this trip to Mexico was planned at the last minute." He paused. "But you can read up on all of that before you board the plane."

"Okay, what is my part? Just follow her?"

"No, you need to get cozy. Kayleigh is flying into Mexico for a museum-quality antique and then escorting it back to New York by van. She'll have to go through customs, and our plan is to stop her there and offer her a deal if she'll turn on London."

Tru sat back. "So why do I need to get cozy?"

"We want you to make sure she reaches the border. Charm her into asking you to tag along. That artifact is a priceless stolen Aztec artifact." Keys clacked again. "Like I said, read the file. We're pretty sure you'll want this one."

"Will do." Tru stood, slipped his belt in the loops, and fastened it. "Is she still near the coffee shop?"

"Yeah, she seems to be sticking to that area."

"All right. Talk later."

Tru ended the call and stood. Maybe he could find Kayleigh and strike up a conversation before they boarded their flight. If not, coffee sounded good, and maybe it would keep him awake and ready for small talk.

He pulled up her photo again, noting the stick-straight blond hair and light brown eyes framed by soft-pink metal-framed glasses. Now that he was studying the picture with zero distraction, he struggled with Ryder's description of a cold-blooded murderer.

With a swipe of his finger, he pulled up the next page and slowly took his seat again. The little boy in the picture...painful memories flooded him. This baby needed the justice Tru and his family never received. The boy's parents couldn't be brought back, but maybe knowing the killer was punished for the crime would help him process it when he got older.

The rest of the file didn't matter. Standing, Tru put

purpose behind his steps and went looking for Kayleigh. After his fifth lap of the merchant area, he was beyond frustrated and in no mood to strike up a conversation with anyone, let alone one that would get him cozy with a killer.

Instead of making a sixth lap, he stopped at the first coffee shop he found and stepped into a line that snaked out the entrance. He pulled out his phone and took the opportunity to familiarize himself with all the details of the case.

NYPD had approached Guardian Group—Tru's employer, a private security company run by his boss, Noah Wolf—with the suspicion of a mole within their department after several sting operations had failed to result in the capture of the Beacon Art Gallery owner, London Carter. The seizure of a hedge fund CEO's storage facility in upstate New York had netted a large private collection of stolen art and antiquities. Part of the man's plea deal had turned them onto London as the one who'd procured the items for him.

The department had devoted countless man-hours to trying to catch her, and as a last resort, they'd reached out for help in not only stopping London, but the mole as well. It had been Noah's call to try a different approach and go after Kayleigh. With her body count, he thought they could flip her and, in turn, take London down too.

"Sir?"

Tru jerked his head up and stuffed his phone into his pocket before placing his order for black coffee with a shot of espresso. A few moments later, his name was called, and he shuffled to the condiment bar, adjusted his duffle bag, and doctored his coffee with a little cream and sugar. Once it was a degree below tongue-blistering hot, he lifted the cup to take a sip.

Just as he put the cup to his lips and tipped it up, a body slammed into him. All at once, the lid popped off his coffee, dumping it onto his face as a shock of hot liquid drenched the front of his clothing.

Before he could reign himself in, he growled, "Watch where you're going!" He spread his arms, still dazed, and tried to process what had taken place. "Geez."

"I am so, so, so, so sorry." A woman's voice trembled as the apology whooshed out almost as if she'd said it all in one word.

All he could see was a blur of dainty hands as coffee dripped off his eyelashes. He heard the distinct sound of paper being pulled from a dispenser right before she began dabbing his shirt.

"I'm so sorry. I'm such a klutz sometimes."

The stain on his shirt was spreading in every direction and dripping down the leg of his jeans. "Great."

Good thing he'd listened to his gut and packed a few extra pieces of clothing in his duffle bag.

She grabbed a few more napkins, and her hands moved down his shirt until she reached his belt. "I got my coffee, and someone bumped into me. I didn't..."

Her gaze lifted to his, and the world stood still. Kayleigh Kingston, wide-eyed with a blanket of pink covering her cheeks. The picture had failed to do her justice. In person, she was beyond beautiful, and despite his current predicament, he couldn't curb the intense feeling that she wasn't guilty, even more so now that he'd come face-to-face with her.

The second her hands reached his belt, the realization that they might go lower hit him and he barked, "Stop." The words came out harsher than expected because he just wanted to prevent her hands from wandering lower. He relaxed his posture and worked to control his voice. "Stop, please."

For a split second, she froze, her mouth opening and closing like she wanted to reply, and then she darted out of the shop faster than he thought someone could move. He exhaled heavily and held in a groan. Not only was his shirt drenched, but he was pretty sure he'd blown his chance to get cozy with his target.

With another huff, he strode to the nearest restroom to clean up. No way was he spending the rest of his day in stained clothing. Normally, he wouldn't use the family restroom, but he felt he had a good excuse this time. Someone his size needed more space than a single stall bathroom to move around in. Once he'd changed his clothes, he left and walked to the men's restroom to wash up.

As he was air-drying his hands, his phone rang. He raked his hand down the length of his now clean jeans and answered, "Hey, Ryder." Most likely he'd picked up Kayleigh's cell signal while they were in the coffee shop.

"Seems like you've already made contact with our suspect. How'd it go?"

Tru grunted. "Before or after she doused me in hot coffee?"

"What?" Ryder laughed.

"One minute I'm drinking coffee; the next minute, I'm drenched in coffee so hot I could sue. I think I've got first-degree burns." He sighed. "Okay, not that bad, but let's just say my first encounter didn't go so great."

"Gotcha. Glad I got you a seat next to her." He paused a second. "And now you're in first class. You can offer her the upgraded seat, which will seem like a nice gesture. Maybe it'll help smooth things over easier."

Tru cleared his throat. "What if she declines the invitation?"

"Good point. I'll keep an eye on the flight, and after

she passes through the gate, I'll make sure the flight is overbooked by one, with her seat being double-booked. Then there won't be a choice."

"That'll help, but won't it be odd that there's an extra seat next to me that just happens to be available?" Even a lie needed to make sense.

Ryder gave a small sigh. "You like your space, right?"

"Yeah? So?"

"Just tell her you booked both seats. As much as you hate lying, that's one less you'll have to tell."

With a grunt, Tru laughed. "You have a point." He raked his hand through his hair, checked himself in the mirror one last time, and left the bathroom. "Hey, Ryder, we're sure Kayleigh is involved, right?"

"Unless we're getting bad intel, then, yeah, she is."

"But you've done that before, right?" Tru had spent enough time with the members of the Guardian Group to know how Noah met his wife, Mia. In the process of keeping close to her, Noah had fallen hard for her.

"Mia, but that was different. They were setting Noah up." Ryder took a deep breath. "Kayleigh has had at least three people killed in three different states. Plus, an eyewitness. She might look innocent, but she's not."

Tru pictured Kayleigh in his mind. "I don't know. I just...my gut says something's not right." So far, it hadn't let him down, either. Even as short as the encounter was, he couldn't shake the feeling.

Groaning, Ryder replied, "Look, don't pull a Noah."

In the background, Mia said, "Hey! I was innocent!"

"We know that now…" Ryder laughed. "Seriously, just watch yourself. We know full well that looks can be deceiving."

A valid argument. One Tru couldn't deny. "I know, and I will."

"Good."

"Okay, talk later." Tru ended the call and stuffed his phone back in his pocket. Now he just needed to wait for the flight. By then, he would hopefully have a plan put together that would get him back in Kayleigh's good graces enough that he could keep tabs on her.

2

*B*roken glasses, her skirt was a mess, and now she didn't even have coffee? Could her day get any worse? She struck a line through the thought and looked upward. "Not a challenge," she whispered.

Thoughts swirled in Kayleigh Kingston's head as she held her skirt up to the air dryer. The edges of the dark brown circle became more pronounced the longer she held it there. Good thing it was long and flowy. Maybe that would hide the stain until she reached the hotel in Mexico City. Why hadn't she listened to her sister's advice to bring a carry-on with an extra outfit?

The coffee shop scene played in her mind again, and she softly groaned. Oh, it was so embarrassing. Not only had she spilled her coffee on the biggest man she'd ever seen, but then she'd tried to clean it up.

Only, she'd been a little too ambitious and nearly touched parts of him she was sure he didn't want a stranger touching.

The strangest part was that she couldn't remember how it happened. Not because of one of her typical blackouts, but because it happened so quickly.

One second she was picking up her coffee, excited about her first time flying, and the next, *wham*...coffee cleanup on aisle Mr. Ginormous. If she hadn't been such a klutz, not only would she be stain-free, but maybe he wouldn't have looked at her so menacingly. If looks could have killed, she'd have been dead and buried six times by now.

She couldn't blame him, though. Poor guy. That coffee was so hot, and she'd poured it all over him and his parts. Her only hope was that his jeans were thick enough to keep him from getting burned too much. Maybe if she saw him again, she could apologize even more profusely. She grimaced. Or maybe not. It was a miracle she'd been able to get her mouth to work the first time. Scratch that. Coffee-covered or not, he was so attractive she would have been tongue-tied either way.

Her phone rang, and she dropped her skirt long enough to fish it out of her purse. London Carter, her boss's name, lit up the caller ID. "Hey, London." She'd keep her little morning misfortune to herself. With her history, the less her boss knew, the better.

Those mistakes were the only reason she'd agreed to fly to Mexico City alone and drive back to New York with a large piece of Aztec statuary. The hotel London had booked her was sketchy too, but she'd lacked the courage to argue. She needed to make it up to London.

So far, Kayleigh's job at the Beacon Art Gallery was the best job she'd ever had, and at nearly a year, it was the longest job she'd held in her twenty-eight years. When she thought of it like that, it sounded horrible. But she'd wanted to experience different things in life. It had just taken her a while to find what she loved— and she loved Beacon Art Gallery.

"Hi. Kayleigh, do you know where my laptop is? I can't find it this morning."

"Uh, no. The last time I saw it, it was on your desk." Kayleigh almost sighed in relief because she knew she hadn't touched it. Since starting work for the gallery, she'd made a ton of mistakes, but London had been so kind and gracious each time. She was one of the reasons Kayleigh loved the job so much.

It had only happened once, but Kayleigh had accidentally taken the gallery laptop home when she first started working there. Her laptop looked almost identical to London's, but she'd taken care of that issue by decorating hers with a few bright stickers. Since then, there had never been another mistake.

"Kayleigh, it's not here. Would you check your bag please?"

"Sure," she replied, squatting down and unzipping her laptop bag. "I have my laptop, but I—" She stopped short, holding in a gasp as her heart dropped to her stomach. It wasn't her laptop. "Uh…"

"Let me guess. You accidentally took mine?" London's sharp voice nearly made Kayleigh jump.

Her heart climbed into her throat as her eyes misted over. "But I didn't. I know I didn't. I have no idea how it got in my bag. I have stickers on mine now to distinguish them."

Before getting the job at the gallery, she'd gone more than a year without any blackouts or memory loss. Shortly after working there, they'd started again. It wouldn't have made sense to her, but the job was stressful, which was typically a trigger for them.

This time? She was sure she hadn't taken it, and she had no idea how it got into her bag. Right as she was supposed to get off work the day before, she'd juggled a delivery, taken several back-to-back calls, and double-checked her itinerary. She'd been in London's office right before she left, but that was after she packed up to leave.

"But you were distracted yesterday before you left."

"I was, but I'd already put away my laptop. I just don't understand how this happened."

London let out a scoff. "I needed that laptop. It has a client's number on it, and they were expecting a call from me today. Lucky for you, they called me this morning while I was in the office. How many times do I have to tell you to be careful, Kayleigh?"

"I'm sorry. I don't know how it happened. I can delay my flight—"

"No, that piece *has* to be picked up on time and escorted back to the states. I've told you how important this trip is. It isn't just some gallery display. It's museum-quality." Not to mention the van reservation. If Kayleigh didn't make it to Mexico City on time, there was a good chance she'd lose it because of the festival being held.

Kayleigh hung her head. "I'm so sorry." How could she have messed up again this badly? "I've been so careful lately."

"Your excuses aren't cutting it anymore." Kayleigh could picture London pinching the bridge of her nose as she spoke. "Look, I feel like I've been more than patient with you, but I just can't keep overlooking your mistakes."

"London, this makes no sense. Our bags look nothing alike. You saw me with my bag, and you know I had my laptop in it."

Another frustrated sigh. "I know you have a habit of being disorganized and forgetful. How many times have you recalled things wrong? Remember the missing painting?"

That was true. Kayleigh still wasn't clear on how it happened, but she'd lost a Picasso that was being loaned to the gallery from a private collector. It had taken hours of work and tons of phone calls, but Kayleigh tracked it down in a little more than a week. It was her last big mistake. "But I found it. And I still don't know how that one happened either."

"Exactly." London huffed. "I'm putting my foot down this time. If you can't make it back to the States with my laptop and the artifact, I'll be forced to fire you. I'm sorry, Kayleigh, but this is the last straw."

She rolled her lips in, forcing back tears. "I love my job. I've been doing so great. It's been a couple of months since anything has happened." She closed the bag and stood. "Please, I'll try even harder."

"You say that every time, and every time, something else happens. There are no more chances." With the last word, the line went dead.

For a moment, Kayleigh looked at the phone in stunned disbelief. London had never spoken to her so harshly. She had a good reason to be upset, but as Kayleigh searched her memory, there wasn't a moment she couldn't account for. She saw London's...

She hung her head as she recalled the scene at the gallery the day before. Right as she was to leave, a rush of customers had walked in, along with several deliveries. Kayleigh had taken care of logging those arrivals into London's laptop. Still, it didn't explain how their laptops got mixed up. That didn't matter, though. London had no reason to believe her. If something was going to go wrong, Kayleigh would be at the root of it.

She squeezed her eyes closed as disappointment filled her. Flighty, forgetful, absentminded, childish… all words attributed to her by just about everyone who knew her. Her two younger sisters were as close to perfect as anyone could get. It's not that her family wasn't loving and supportive, they just wanted more for her.

The reason she'd worked so hard at this job was to show them she could be grounded. To gain a little respect and have stability. And that was exactly what she was going to do. She did have a direction and a plan, and that was to do the best job she could for London.

She pinched her lips together and stood. If London wanted that laptop and the artifact, that's exactly what she was going to get. Kayleigh was keeping her job and proving to herself that she could be counted on. She pulled her laptop bag onto her shoulder, took the handle of her luggage, and marched out of the restroom.

Once she reached the gate, she found a spot out of the way and checked her flight information on her phone again. Near the front, which meant she'd get on the plane last, but on the positive side, she'd be one of the first off. Meaning she wouldn't be using that tiny little room they'd mislabeled as a bathroom, according to some flight reviews she'd read. The only memory she had of one so small was a concert port-a-potty, and that was an experience she never wanted to relive.

A text from her baby sister, Autumn, popped up. Not only were Kayleigh and her sisters close in age, but their relationships were close as well. Autumn was currently doing her residency to become a doctor, and Meesha was in Paris working as a teacher. Which was one of the reasons Kayleigh needed to prove she could keep a job. Her sisters were successful, and she wanted that too.

Good luck on your trip.

Kayleigh let out a sigh.

Thanks. I'll need it. I spilled coffee on a giant.

What?

> Someone bumped into me, and I
> poured coffee all over the biggest guy
> I've ever seen. Seriously, his biceps
> were the size of truck tires.

Ohhh…was he cute?

Rolling her eyes, Kayleigh chuckled. No way was she giving her sister that kind of ammunition.

> I didn't even pay attention. I was so
> embarrassed that I apologized and
> then ran away.

I probably would have done the same thing, but I'd have been with it enough to know if he was cute in case I needed to apologize again.

Well, I didn't.

The announcement of Kayleigh's flight caught her attention. She briefly looked up and then back down to her phone, making sure to listen for her row.

Hey, my plane is boarding. I need to go.

Okay, just be careful, okay? If you need anything, call or text.

I will. Kayleigh waited a beat and then added, *Thanks for the luck.*

Anytime. I love you.

I love you too.

Kayleigh's row was called out over the intercom,

and she walked to the agent, holding her phone under the barcode reader.

The agent smiled and pointed to the tunnel next to her. "Have a good trip. Thanks for flying with us."

"Thanks."

Before she reached the entrance to the plane, three more texts popped up from her sister Meesha, her mom, and her dad, each wishing her a safe trip and telling her they loved her. She quickly replied and then set the phone on plane mode.

A blond stewardess gave her a cheery greeting as she stepped onto the plane. It wasn't until then that it fully hit Kayleigh that she was about to take her first flight ever. Her stomach flipped at the thought. With all her moves, she'd driven because she was packing up her life and it was easier and cheaper to just take it all in her car.

Now that she was actually on the plane, her nerves frazzled a little. Swallowing hard, she forced the thoughts away. This flight was going to be awesome.

She shuffled behind the person in front of her through first class, and her gaze briefly locked with the man she'd spilled coffee on. Jerking her gaze away, she tried to pretend she didn't remember him.

"Uh, hello?"

She dragged her attention back to him. "Hi. I'm—"

The man's lips quirked into the most brilliant, sexy

smile she'd ever seen, rattling her brain and making her lose whatever train of thought she had. "Really, I'm sorry for reacting the way I did. It was just an accident."

A nervous, wobbly laugh popped out. "Yeah, I don't know what happened."

"It's okay, really."

She tucked a piece of hair behind her ear and smiled. "Um, thanks."

His gorgeous smile widened, crinkling the corners of his equally gorgeous blue eyes. Now that he wasn't upset, he was much less intimidating and hotter than a ghost pepper.

The person in front of her moved forward, and she inched past him. "Have a nice flight."

"You too," he said and winked.

Seriously? Winking at her? What was it about that little action that made her knees wobbly? As outward appearances went, he'd just checked more than one of her boxes.

This time, the line really moved and her with it. Now she wished she'd booked first class. Of course, that was what her heart would say. Her bank account heartily disagreed.

When she reached her row, she found all the seats occupied. She pulled up the image on her phone again.

"Uh, my ticket says this is my seat." She smiled at the lady in seat D.

The woman blinked and pulled her paper ticket from the small clutch in her lap. "5D." She held it up. Sure enough, she was right.

This couldn't be happening. Kayleigh had been on time. How had her seat been given away? She looked toward the front of the plane and caught the attention of a flight attendant.

The woman closed as much of the distance as she could. "Yes?"

Kayleigh explained what happened and showed the woman her phone.

The flight attendant's eyebrows knitted together, and she nodded. "Let me see what's going on."

Pressing herself against the edge of the seat, Kayleigh allowed the people behind her to pass.

A few minutes later, the stewardess returned. "I'm so sorry, but this flight is booked. We're going to have to have you go back to the gate and speak to the ticket agent."

"Booked? But..." If she could, she'd just dissolve into a puddle of tears right then and there.

The flight attendant motioned for Kayleigh to follow. With each step, dread built in her stomach. How was she going to explain this to London?

Mr. Ghost-Pepper-Hot gave her a curious look as she passed. "What happened?"

"The flight is overbooked, and I have to leave." She almost got through the entire sentence before her voice faltered.

"Wait." He looked around and moved into the aisle, leaning in. "I hate to admit this in public, but the seat next to me is empty."

"What?" Kayleigh asked.

"When I'm traveling, I like my space, and these flights can get claustrophobic. I usually book two seats. This flight seems to be pretty important, and I'd hate you to miss it just because I like a little more legroom."

The stewardess looked from the hot guy to Kayleigh and back to him.

He pulled out his phone and showed it to her. "See? Two seats."

"Really? You'd give up one of your seats for me? Even after..." Kayleigh let the words trail off. It was embarrassing the first time, and she didn't exactly want to relive it again with even more strangers.

He flashed another great smile. "I wasn't exactly Mr. Congeniality."

Kayleigh chewed her bottom lip as she debated. He was being really nice, but she'd already made the start of his trip horrible. "Uh..."

"Seriously, it's okay. I promise."

The exhale she'd been holding poured out of her. "Oh, thank you so much. I really appreciate it."

What a nice man. She didn't know how she was going to thank him, but somewhere between New York City and their connecting flight in North Carolina, she'd figure out a way to show how appreciative she was.

3

*W*ell, Ryder had come through, and now Kayleigh Kingston was parked next to Tru until they reached Charlottesville. Hopefully, by that time, he would get to know her well enough that she'd let him stick close.

He shook hands with her. "I'm Thaddeus Turner, but most people just call me Tru." Ryder hadn't just given him a false identity both on paper in the form of a driver's license and a digital one. The nickname had been scrubbed, so he felt safe using it.

"Kayleigh Kingston." Turning to him, she said, "Thank you so much for letting me take one of your seats." She placed her hand on his forearm before jerking it back and shaking out her fingers. "Oh! Static electricity."

He'd felt the little pop too, but he wasn't so sure it

was static as much as just electricity that raced through his hand and up his arm. An odd feeling he'd yet to experience with a woman. "You're okay, and I don't mind. I have plenty of space." Even if he hadn't, he still wouldn't mind. Despite knowing she was a criminal, he was intrigued by her.

Now that he wasn't covered in coffee, he was able to appreciate just how cute she was. Beautiful could apply as well, and her nervousness made her charming.

"Where are you headed?" she asked.

"Mexico City. You?" The obvious follow-up to her question.

Her eyes twinkled as she grinned. "Me too. I can see why you'd want space. You're huge." She flattened her hand against his bicep. "It's bigger than my hand." Again, she jerked her hand away. "I am so sorry. I promise I will stop touching you. When I get nervous, my brain takes a minute to catch up with the rest of me. It happens all the time. Busses, trains, planes... apparently, and then..." She clamped her lips shut. "I ramble too."

Tru shook his head as he laughed. Definitely adorable. He leaned in a little closer, smiling. "Why are you nervous?" What was he doing? Yeah, he was supposed to be cozying up to her, but flirting? That was leading her on and worse than lying. Criminal or not, that wasn't okay in his book, and he wasn't that type of guy.

Her eyes widened as her cheeks bloomed dark red. "Uh…" The word came out breathy. It was interesting to see the effect he had on her. Another new experience for him. A quirk he'd noticed.

What was it about an attractive woman blushing that ticked his boxes? Maybe because he'd been a bodyguard for numerous women who knew they were beautiful, and the ones who didn't know made it easy to be around them. "You really don't need to be nervous around me."

"Yeah, well…" The words trailed off, but he could've sworn she said he was drop-dead gorgeous. Three words he'd never associated himself with. He wasn't hideous, he didn't think, but he was okay with calling himself average.

The plane began taxiing away from the terminal, and the two stewardesses took their places to go over the safety procedures. On most of his flights, Tru tried to put himself near the escape hatches. Most people who flew had no idea what they'd do in an emergency because they'd never been trained to face them. With his background, it only made sense to take on the responsibility.

Resting his head on the back of the seat, Tru closed his eyes. This was typically the time he'd rest his eyes until he reached his destination. Plus, he didn't want to seem overeager to talk to Kayleigh. He'd learned very early on that letting a target come to him was the best way to catch them.

As the plane began to jiggle from the takeoff, arms snaked around his in a gorilla grip, jerking his attention to Kayleigh. "Are you okay?" he asked.

"Never flown before." The words came out strangled.

Never flown before? That didn't track with what they knew. She'd committed several murders all over the country. Unless she was just a great actor, which was completely possible. If that was how she was playing it though, he'd take her lead.

He covered one of her hands with his. "Hey, it's okay. This is all normal."

Just as the plane's wheels began to retract, she buried her face in his arm. She was shaking nearly as badly as the plane. This woman needed to be on Broadway. It was the best performance he'd ever seen.

Her tight hold on him didn't lessen until they'd nearly reached their cruising altitude, and by then, he was wondering if he'd get circulation back in his arm.

Finally, she leaned back, tears pooling in her eyes, and said, "Is it always like that?"

So scared she didn't hear him tell her that? Possible,

he guessed. "Yeah, it is." He studied her a moment. "You've never flown before?"

Shaking her head, she peeled her arms from around him and hugged herself. "No. I've always driven wherever I wanted to go."

Tru knew what the file said, but his gut was telling him something wasn't right. He'd been around plenty of guilty people trying to act innocent, and they'd never been this convincing. "Where all have you lived?"

"Mostly small towns." She turned to him. "Most people go to the big cities. They think all the adventure is there, but small towns have so much to offer."

"But you're in New York City now."

She lowered her gaze, tucking a piece of hair behind her ear. "Yeah, I thought I was madly in love and moved here to be closer to my boyfriend at the time. He was a musician traveling through the town I was in, and we hit it off and…" She rolled her lips in.

"And?" he asked, interested in the rest of the sentence.

"He said I was a gifted guitarist. That he loved my songs." She sighed. "But…" Shaking her head, she waved him off. "Anyway, again, thank you for the seat, and I'll leave you alone now."

The fasten-seat-belt sign dinged off, and the captain spoke, giving his name and their altitude and thanking them for flying. As soon as he was finished, Tru said, "What if I don't want to be left alone?" He chuckled.

This time her blush went all the way to her ears. He needed to stop flirting, but it was so easy with her.

Her lips quirked into a smile, and she pulled her gaze from his and up to the controls overhead, opening the air vent a little more. "It's warmer in here than I thought it would be."

When was the last time he'd met a woman so easy to be around? He chuckled. "You play guitar and write songs?" His job was to get details, not get friendly. While these details didn't help the case, they did pave the way for deeper questions.

Nodding, she fidgeted with her fingers. "Yeah, I play piano too."

"Wow, piano and guitar? You're really talented, then." He was genuinely impressed. Again, questions floated to mind about her guilt. But criminals could be talented in things other than breaking the law, so it wasn't so farfetched to think she could play instruments or write songs. For all he knew, this was her cover and she was great at playing the part of an innocent woman.

"They're just hobbies. My two younger sisters are the talented ones. They have their ducks in rows, and I can't even find mine." She laughed, but the tone was stoic.

The war going on between Tru's head and heart were giving him a headache. This woman was a murderer and a thief. And a liar as well. There was no mention of siblings at all in her file, and Tru knew Ryder and Mia well enough to know they wouldn't have missed something like that.

Kayleigh had taken a job at Beacon Art Gallery under the employ of London Carter. Even if Kayleigh confessed that her boss put her up to it, it wouldn't change the charges. She might be able to make a deal for turning on London, but that wouldn't absolve her of guilt.

Twisting in her seat, she faced Tru, and he was struck by how golden her eyes were. A smile lifted one corner of her lips. "How about you? Any hobbies?"

"I love history." It was the story they'd developed as to why he was flying to Mexico City, and it kept him from lying because it was actually true. He loved the gun range too, but that wasn't always the best detail to share. "Old books, ruins, all of it."

"Really?" She blinked. "I can't say I expected that answer."

"Why?" He tilted his head.

"No good reason. I'm guilty of judging your cover." The words came out like she was disappointed in herself.

He laughed. "Everyone does that."

She lifted an eyebrow. "Oh really? Then what did you think about my cover?"

Shaking his head, he grinned. "I'm a lot of things, but I'm not stupid enough to walk into traps."

"I won't hold it against you." She caught his gaze and held it.

His mouth went dry as the air grew warm around him. "I think you're beautiful, and the way you carry yourself makes me smile." It had all just tumbled out like his brain wasn't switched on. He was undercover, trying to catch a bad guy—her. Not looking for a girlfriend.

Her lips parted slightly with a small gasp. "I definitely won't hold that against you. Most of the time, I'm sticking my foot in my mouth or rambling or…any other number of annoying things. I'm twenty-eight, and I'm constantly told to act my age."

The ten-year age gap gave him pause for a split second. It was just a number. "Thirty-eight, and I should probably act less than my age at times. It might help me feel younger longer."

She lowered her gaze, inhaling and then slowly exhaling. "I can see their point. I mean, by now I should have a career, a family, or something I can say I'm building on, but I love trying new things. I don't like staying in one place all the time."

"Did you say you needed this flight for your job?

That's something you love, right?" Maybe this would get her to open up about Beacon. He may not get all the intel, but it would be a starting place. There was always a chance she could slip up and give him a lead to pass on to Ryder.

Lifting her gaze to his, she nodded. "Yeah, I do love it. Somewhat. I mean, I wish…it's dumb." She waved him off.

He touched her hand and then jerked his back. Another pop of electricity coursed through his veins. If the universe was sending him a message that touching her was bad, he was officially on notice. "Tell me anyway."

Kayleigh chewed her bottom lip a second. "It doesn't fit my personality at all, but have you ever watched the show *Chuck* or *Scarecrow and Mrs. King*?"

"Maybe. The name sounds familiar, but I don't watch much television." He smiled. "That last one I know because my grandma loved it. She had the whole series on DVD."

Her face lit up. "Well, I don't have to tell you how great *Scarecrow* was, but *Chuck* was equally great. It followed a regular guy who stumbled into being a spy. I loved it, not just because he was normal, but because he always tried to do what was right." Her smile slowly faded. "He didn't like lying or using people."

This time Tru used the back of his hand to lightly

touch her knee and felt another bolt rocket through him. Clearly, he was a slow learner. "Sounds like a great show, but why the sad face?"

Waving him off, she replied, "Oh, nothing. I just like the idea of the normal, ordinary person put in a position where they can save the world. You know, something bigger than myself." She shrugged. "I do love my job at an art gallery. I get to see so much talent. The paintings, sculptures, and priceless artifacts that come through are amazing. Although, I wish most of it wasn't going to private collectors. It's sealed away from the rest of the world, and it seems a shame to me."

It was more than that, but he wouldn't press it, especially since he had no idea what was true or not. "I feel the same way. History should be for everyone. To see how people lived and worked centuries ago. It's a tragedy that so much history is stowed away in private collections rather than on display for the world." Selling a cover was so much easier when it wasn't a lie. He didn't need to force the passion he felt when he was telling the truth.

"See? That's how I feel. Several of our artifacts have come from Mexico, and I look at them and wonder what life must have been like. It's just a shame."

"Does your employer ever display the items before they're sold?"

Shaking her head, she sighed. "No, most of the time they're already sold before they even arrive. It's only in the last month or so that my boss let me check them in. At first, I didn't even know we got those types of items. Much of the artwork we have is from current artists. Although, we've displayed a few paintings from Picasso, Salvador Dali, and others. They weren't there long because those were typically loaned from museums."

Finding a woman who loved history as much as he did was a rare thing. Of course, he'd dated a few who loved going to art galleries, but it wasn't about the history; it was more just a place to go. Then reality rushed back. This woman was feeding him lies, and even if she was passionate about history, she was still a criminal.

A little voice in the back of his mind screamed, *Innocent until proven guilty*, but he pushed it away. Even if that were true, that Kayleigh was innocent, eventually she'd find out who he was and why he'd been so nice. Not only did he need to remember she was a killer and a thief, but he needed to remember that even if she weren't, she was off-limits.

4

Oh my goodness, I got to sit next to him in first class. Kayleigh furiously typed out the text and sent it to her sister Autumn.

Sitting in first class wasn't something Kayleigh had experienced before. Even as a first-time flyer, she knew anything less would be a letdown in the future. Based on the movies she'd watched, she'd been expecting cramped seats and being squished between two people who snored. Then add Tru who was attractive, charming, and kind. Next time wouldn't live up to her first venture.

He'd even invited her to eat with him during their layover, but she hadn't wanted to infringe on him more than she already had. It was sweet, and it had been difficult to say no.

Not a second later, Autumn's text popped up. *The guy you spilled coffee on?*

Somehow my flight was overbooked. He'd booked two seats and offered to let me take one of them so I didn't miss my flight.

EEEEEEE! So you spill coffee on him and then he offers you a seat? That's so serendipitous. Are you still hanging out with him? Did he ask you out? Did you exchange numbers?

No, no, and no. He was just being nice because he felt bad that he was grouchy. We talked during the flight, though. He's... What should she say? Dreamy? Because he was. The little glint in his eyes when he flirted with her, the way he looked at her...and she found herself completely comfortable around him.

The same things she'd said about her ex-boyfriend. That relationship had burned out just as fast as it started. She'd trusted Kip too, and he'd ended up stealing her songs.

Kayleigh deleted *He's* and began typing again. *He was sweet, but I need to keep my feet on the ground. I have a job I love and want to keep. I need to focus on that.*

She was too embarrassed to tell her sister about the laptop and the threat of losing her job. London Carter was a sore subject between them already. Autumn didn't care for Kayleigh's boss at all.

You can multitask. LOL!

Do you remember who you're talking to? I took out a mailbox because I can't talk and drive at the same time. Seriously, Autumn, you and Meesha have such great lives. Mom and Dad are so proud of you. I want that.

After roughly a minute with no reply, Kayleigh sighed and forged ahead from the gate and began to look for a place to eat. Would it have hurt to have a meal with Tru? She could have paid for his meal as a way to say thank you. Too late now. They'd parted at the gate after a little bit of small talk. It had been a sign that he'd only offered to eat together because it was the polite thing to do.

Her phone dinged, and she read Autumn's text. *Kayleigh, Mom and Dad are proud of you. They want you to be happy. It wasn't your fault. We're just glad we still have you. We love you just the way you are. It's okay. You make us laugh. You keep us from being boring.*

A lump formed in her throat. They always tried to make her feel better, and it was sweet. They just didn't understand.

"Why are you looking so sad?"

Tru's voice caught her off guard, and as she whirled to face him, her feet tangled. Just as she thought dental work would be in her future, he wrapped his arms around her and steadied her. "Whoa. Sorry. I didn't mean to startle you."

All she could do was stare at him for a moment

before her wits returned. "I'm so sorry." The words rushed out breathy.

"I don't know. I think I got a good deal. A beautiful woman in my arms." He smiled. Sheesh. If charm were a sport, he'd have a blue ribbon.

She stepped back, tucking a piece of hair behind her ear. "Uh." For a second, she debated with herself and then quickly asked, "I think I owe you lunch. First you give me your seat, and then you keep me from breaking my face."

"I don't want you to think you owe me for anything. I was in the right place at the right time." He turned, and she quickly grabbed his arm.

"No, really, I'd love to buy you lunch." And keep listening to that voice. Deep and warm and goose-bump-inducing.

He held her gaze, and butterflies fluttered in her stomach enough that she nearly laughed as they tickled her. His eyebrows scrunched together. "Are you sure? It's really no big deal—"

"No, I insist. Please." She touched his arm.

"Okay." He shot her a cute lopsided grin. Whoa. That was a good one too. "What sounds good?"

Kayleigh's butterfly-filled stomach suddenly growled. "Pretzels and beer cheese always sounds good to me, but—"

His mouth dropped open. "No way. Everywhere I

go, I try to find a place so I can try them. The best I've ever had was in Garden City, Kansas. Little restaurant there had such a funky atmosphere, and the food was delicious."

"Really?" She couldn't believe it. "I do the same thing. Everywhere. Sometimes, though, I bomb hard."

"No kidding, and when it's bad…"

"It's really bad," they said in unison and laughed.

Be still her beating heart. He loved history and pretzels with beer cheese. Had the universe finally smiled down on her and sent her a good guy?

Probably not. As much as she wanted it, she really did need to focus on keeping her job. She didn't want to move back home with her tail tucked between her legs. She needed to be working for something, a better future. No guy wanted a girl who, at her age, didn't have her life together. At least somewhat.

He lifted his gaze and tipped his chin toward the far end of the airport. "I'd decided to just grab a sandwich instead of sitting down to eat. There was a place over there that smelled really good. How about that?"

Shrugging, she nodded. "Sure."

They walked in silence to the restaurant and found it not too busy. It helped because their plane had landed a little after ten. The host took them to their seats and left them with menus.

"Well, that stinks. No pretzels and cheese." Tru

heaved a heavy sigh. "High hopes crash hard." He laughed.

"Whatever they're cooking sure smells good, doesn't it?" She hadn't realized how hungry she was until then. "I think I could eat leather, I'm so hungry."

He looked down at the menu and back up. "How about we share some chips and queso? Maybe we can make better decisions if we aren't starving."

Their waiter stopped at their table and took their drink and appetizer order, giving them a little more time to make a selection.

As Tru looked over the menu, he said, "I'm torn between seafood and a burger."

There were plenty of choices, and it was a hard decision. "I'm going for the Montecristo sandwich." That was something she liked to try at different places too.

"Oh, I like those." He looked at her. "Now I have an even harder choice."

She braced her hands on her seat and leaned forward a little. "We could each get something and share it. That way we can try both things."

He nodded. "Sounds good to me. What do you want to try?"

Kayleigh looked down at the menu. The prices were pretty high, but she could splurge a little, especially for the guy who'd helped her keep her job. "Sea bass with asparagus and cream sauce?"

"You speak my language." The corners of his eyes creased as his lips lifted into a brilliant wide grin.

Breathe, Kayleigh, breathe. Boy, was he charming, and the longer she was around him, the better-looking he got, if that were even possible.

When the waiter returned, he set their drinks and appetizer on the table, took their orders, and they were left alone again. The silence stretched out until Tru took a sip of his drink and cleared his throat. "So, tell me more about your job."

"Beacon Art Gallery in New York City. My boss, London Carter, has been in business for thirty years. She's been so good to me." Kayleigh's smile faltered a moment. "I'm a klutz and very forgetful sometimes, and she's been more than patient with me."

His head tilted. "I doubt you're that bad."

She groaned, not wanting to tell this gorgeous man she was a walking, talking Murphy's Law. But it was the truth, and it was better for him to know now rather than later. Perhaps a warning would keep him from getting coffee spilled on him again.

"Awful. The first month I was there, I accidentally took the gallery's laptop home—London's, if I'm being precise. Didn't even realize it until the next day when London was looking for it. Had no idea we had the exact same laptop. I haven't broken vases or anything, thank goodness, but I did lose a painting for about two weeks a few months ago."

"How did you lose it? Or I guess the better question is, how did you find it?"

"Somehow I'd gotten the clients mixed up and sent it to the wrong person. Took me a couple of weeks to track it down, but I got it back."

"That's good." He leaned forward with his arms on the table. "Sounds like you fixed it."

Nodding, she said, "I thought London would be furious, but she wasn't." Kayleigh had fully expected to be fired, but instead, London had told her that mistakes happen. It was how they were fixed that mattered. "I could tell she was upset, of course, but she just looked me in the eyes and told me she knew I could find it."

Kayleigh exhaled softly. "It was the first time I felt like someone cared about me." She rolled her eyes. "I mean, someone other than my family. She had faith in me that I could make it right."

"Sounds like a fantastic boss."

"She really is. That's the reason I'm headed to Mexico City, to pick up art. I'm escorting it back to New York to pay her back for all her patience." Kayleigh chewed the inside of her cheek a second. "So, what do you do?"

"I'm a history professor at a small two-year college in Denver. I flew into JFK a few days ago so I could see Cats before heading to Mexico City to see the Palace of the Plumed Butterfly."

She hadn't expected that as an answer. Bodyguard, bouncer, Greek god, sure, but teacher? "I wasn't expecting that."

A deep, rich laughter poured from him. "I get that a lot."

"You're just so...big."

"I was kidding. I retired from the Marines, and now I teach self-defense classes."

Kayleigh leaned back, shaking her head. "I'm so sorry for stereotyping you."

Shrugging, he held his hand to his mouth as he coughed. "It's really okay. I mean, people see me, and it's easy to expect that."

"I guess I fit a stereotype too. Glasses, blond hair, goofy."

Tru stared at her a moment. "I don't think so. You work for a gallery. Now, if you'd said waitress or something, maybe." He held up his hands. "Not that there is anything wrong with that. Just saying, what you do isn't stereotypical."

Before she could respond, the waiter returned with their food, setting it on the table in front of them. Her stomach growled as the aroma hit her nose. "Oh, if it tastes anything like it smells..."

"Thank you," Tru said to the waiter. "This looks great."

The waiter nodded. "Good. I'll be back to fill up your glasses in a moment."

Tru forked a flake of the fish off, cooling it a bit, and then ate it. He moaned. "Wow. This is delicious." He pushed his plate in her direction. "That sandwich looks like it could give you third-degree burns. This one isn't too bad if you blow on it."

As much as she wanted to dig into her food, she was with Tru. It was still sizzling. She did just as he'd done before, pulling off a piece with her fork and blowing on it before popping it into her mouth. She moaned just as loud or louder than him. "Ohhhhh... this is fantastic."

"No kidding." He pulled off another bite, more generous than the last. "Maybe I should have ordered two."

"Maybe." She cut off a piece of her sandwich and took a bite. "Oh, yeah, definitely two." Then she sliced off some and placed it on Tru's plate. "To die for."

He picked it up and ate it, nodding. "Oh, man."

She laughed. "Best airport food I've ever had."

"I thought you've never flown before."

With a roll of her eyes, she said, "Meaning it's the

only airport food I've ever had, so of course it's the best."

Shaking his head, he exhaled heavily. "That was a *duh* moment."

"So…is there a girlfriend who will want to beat me up for having lunch with you?" The words were out of her mouth before she could stop them. "Guess I should have asked that a lot sooner."

"No, there's no girlfriend, and I wouldn't be sitting here if there was." He took a sip of his drink. "I think men can have friends who are women, but they need to show respect to their significant others so there's no room for suspicion."

"Good answer." She smiled.

His head dropped back as he laughed. He looked at her. "I guess that did sound rather diplomatic."

"Very much so. But it's nice to know you'd respect someone you were dating." Her heart skipped a beat as his gaze caught hers. She broke eye contact and took another bite of her food. No, this time she wasn't going to get distracted by a man, especially when London was putting so much trust in her.

They quietly finished their lunch, and once they were finished, Tru opened his wallet.

"No way! I'm paying." She quickly dug in her purse, pulling out her card. "You've already done enough. This was my treat."

"I'm just leaving the tip."

Shaking her head, she said, "No, I've got it. Really."

His shoulders sagged as he sighed. "Fine." He shoved his wallet back in his pocket. "Thank you. I appreciate it." His phone dinged, and he pulled it out of his shirt pocket. "Uh, I really have to take this."

"Sure. This was nice. Thank you."

He stood, holding his duffle bag. "Maybe I'll see you on the plane. Have a great trip, okay?"

"You too."

With a small wave, he strode to the exit, and she watched him leave. It was official, though, she liked his back as much as she liked his front. She took a deep breath. This was good. She'd had lunch with him, and that was all there was to it.

Silently, she commended herself for keeping her head on her shoulders. In the past, she would have nearly begged to stick close to Tru, but this time, she'd held steady. For once, she was proud of herself. It was only one step, but at least it was in the right direction.

5

*A*fter a quick trip to the restroom, Tru found an out-of-the-way spot and put the phone to his ear. "Hey, Ryder."

"Hey. So, how did it go?"

"Uh, we had lunch. She told me about the gallery and London. She's confirmed she's escorting a piece back to New York."

"Good."

More like great. And the first time he'd sat across from a woman in a while. Kayleigh was sweet and funny, and he was drawn to her unlike anyone he'd met before. No matter how many times he reminded himself she was a criminal, he struggled to believe it. She was clumsy and bubbly, and he liked her. The little bit they'd talked only made him want more. He liked being around her. It made the small battle that had started in the coffee shop much larger.

Not only did they share a love of history, but a love of food. He couldn't believe it when she said she wanted pretzels and beer cheese. Her suggestion to order different entrees and share was something he loved doing. It was like the woman had been picked out just for him. A little cruel, really, when he thought about the situation he was in.

Tru hesitated a minute and then said, "I...I just don't think she's capable. My gut still says something is off."

The clacking of keys sounded through the phone. "Then your gut is way off. While you were walking around in the airport, she was calling out a hit on the guys she's meeting tomorrow. She wants there to be no one who can place her there."

How could Tru have been so wrong? Was she really able to pretend innocence so well that he'd buy it? She did say their lunch was the best airport food she'd ever had. Then she'd said it was because she'd never had airport food before. Still, he couldn't shake the weird feeling. Murderer and Kayleigh just didn't fit together. "Do we know who she's using?" he asked, leaning his shoulder against the wall.

"Some small gang there. There's a wire transfer set up to deposit as soon as she's provided confirmation that the hit's taken place." He paused a second. "We're notifying the Mexico City police so they step in before the hit takes place."

"Okay." Tru needed to just focus on his job. His gut feeling needed to be muted until this was all over. His desire to find his perfect match was clouding his judgment. Another reason relationships didn't go well with his job, and another reason he'd eventually have to choose between career and family. For now, he had to stay clear-headed and stick to the job. "I just left her at the restaurant. I'm trying to keep it from being obvious. I figured I'd bump into her again once we reach Mexico City."

"That's a good idea." More keyboard clicks. "She reserved a work van for when she gets there. I'm waiting to switch her reservation to your name until later. I don't want her getting an email and then trying to get a vehicle somewhere else. Even if it would be hard because of the festival that runs the entire week. I don't want someone canceling and her getting a call."

"Okay." Tru shifted on his feet and rolled against the wall onto his back. "Any provisions?"

"Yeah, a duffle bag with weapons and ammunition, a first aid kit, and camping equipment. Not that I think you'll need the latter, but I'm going with better safe than sorry."

"Good call. What about the next connection? Will I be sitting next to her again?"

Ryder cleared his throat. "No, don't want it to look too obvious, but I've got you a hotel room next to hers. It's not at the one she booked. Most likely, she'll be getting a call from the original hotel saying they were booked and they're offering to upgrade her to another hotel."

"What was wrong with the one she booked?"

"According to Hendrix, it isn't the best area for tourists."

Coming from Hendrix, that meant something. They'd served together in the Marines and had been in places that seemed to try to one-up each other in terms of unsanitary conditions. "Oh, yeah, I don't think she would have liked that. Nor would I."

Laughing, Ryder said, "Yeah, well, I got a street view the other day, and I can't be positive, but the sludge spilling out of the front door didn't look like water."

That seabass Tru had eaten was trying to make a run for it. He held his stomach. "Stop. That's disgusting."

"Which is why I got you reservations at another hotel. No parking provided by the hotel, but they do have a valet service. Just to keep you from wasting your time looking for a place to park."

"Thanks."

Ryder grunted. "Mia is the one who told me to mention it."

Just as he was about to reply, Tru's phone buzzed with another call coming through. He checked the phone and chuckled. Hendrix, no doubt calling Tru to tell him about the hotel upgrade. "Hey, that's Hendrix."

"All right."

Tru exchanged a quick goodbye with Ryder before switching lines. "I know. You got me the hotel upgrade."

"You owe me. That's, what? At least two now."

"Whatever, man." Tru shook his head, rolling his eyes.

"How's your case?"

Confusing? "I guess it's okay."

There was a good pause. "Your gut?"

Raking his hand through his hair, Tru replied, "Something's off. But the intel Ryder has says she's exactly what they say she is. She's called out a hit on the people she's meeting to pick up the antiquity. No loose ends, apparently."

Hendrix inhaled. "Tough. Your gut has never been wrong."

Having never served with him, Ryder didn't understand how many times Tru's intuition had kept his regiment from being ambushed or where a sniper might be. It had never let him down, and he couldn't understand why it was betraying him now. "I know that and you know that, but Guardian Group doesn't. I don't know what to do."

"Yeah, you do."

"Follow orders and let the rest sort itself?" Tru couldn't argue against that. Although, with Hendrix, it was hard sometimes. While Tru had talked some about his family and such, Hendrix was always guarded. But he was a good friend and that's what mattered to Tru.

"Yep. It's like the CO said: yeah, you have instinct, but orders supersede it. We made a promise to follow Noah's orders. If he's wrong, then he'll have to deal with it."

Scrubbing his hand down his face, Tru exhaled. "Yeah, I know." Following Noah's orders had been a job requirement. The first and most important. Tru understood, but in situations like this, it was harder than usual.

"Do your job. If they're right, she needs to be stopped. If they're wrong, they can present the evidence in court and she'll be exonerated. Innocent until proven guilty. But for you, right now, you need to just assume she's guilty. It'll be easier."

"Yeah, thanks, man." Tru's flight announcement came over the loudspeaker. "Oh, hey, I've got to go."

"Good luck. See you when you get back."

"See ya."

Tru ended the call, picked up his pack, and began trekking to the gate. Hendrix was always practical. Do the job and let the facts sort themselves when it was over and done. Honestly, it was the best way to tackle any job. It was too easy to allow feelings to override common sense and get someone in trouble quickly.

Plus, he knew Ryder and Noah well enough that they wouldn't give him bad information. If they said it was true, it was true. How long had it been since he'd been on a date? That was a factor too. His last relationship lasted about six months before the strain of what he did for a living killed it. They'd mutually ended it, but she'd been the one wanting to hang it up.

Maybe what he really needed to be thinking about was what he wanted in life. Did he want a family and kids? If so, did he want to risk his life when he had a family? That seemed the most reasonable thing to do. To figure out what he wanted and then go with it. Law or love. The two weren't compatible.

6

*A*n internal war had waged in Kayleigh's heart and mind since her lunch with Tru ended. Part of her wanted to seek him out and learn all she could about him, and the other said she'd never forgive herself if she lost her job. It was the position she'd held the longest, and she was on the verge of losing it. What did she want? A man or an occupation? Unfortunately, her heart kept asking why she couldn't have both.

She sat in the back of the plane and saw him board. Instead of trying to make eye contact, she ducked her head and read the magazine in the storage compartment in front of her. One look into those blue eyes, and she was going to drown.

Instead of getting off the plane right away when they landed, she waited until it was nearly empty, hoping he hadn't waited for her. Her heart deflated when she made it to the gate and he wasn't there. For the first time in her life, she was more torn than ever. She consoled herself with the fact that after she got back to New York and she'd had a few months with no problems, maybe she'd be open to dating again.

When she reached the car rental company, her shoulders sagged. Of course, Tru would be there. It didn't matter, though. She needed to get her van and get to the hotel she'd booked.

She stepped up to the counter, and Tru grinned. "We seem to keep running into each other," he said.

Pitter-patter went her heart. Had he gotten more attractive since the end of their lunch? Because it sure seemed like it. "Seems so."

The man at the counter greeted her. "Do you have a reservation?"

She held up her phone to show the man her number. "Yep."

He tapped the number into his tablet, and his eyebrows knitted together. "May I see that number again?"

"Sure," she replied, holding the phone up once more.

He tapped them in again. "I'm sorry; I'm not finding it."

Kayleigh held in a frustrated groan. First her flight, and now the van reservation. What on earth was going on? At least London couldn't fault her. Only, she would because London wasn't accepting excuses anymore. "Do you have anything I could rent?"

The man shook his head. "No, I'm sorry. We're having a festival starting tonight, and everything is booked."

"Is that why it was so hard to find hotel reservations?"

"I'm afraid so."

Forcing tears back, she replied, "Okay, thank you."

Turning from the counter, she palmed her forehead before walking to the nearest bench and taking a seat. Her rear barely hit the solid surface before the tears began running down her cheeks. How was she ever to get her life together if nothing ever worked out for her? She had a plane reservation; it was overbooked. She had a car reservation; it was lost.

Her phone rang, and she recognized the number to the hotel she'd booked. Maybe they had a shuttle and could help her find another van to hold the artifact she was picking up the next day.

"Hello?"

"Hello," a woman with a thick accent answered. "I'm so sorry, but it seems there was a mix-up and we're—"

Kayleigh's heart raced. "Please do not tell me you don't have a room for me."

"No, *señorita*, we do not have a room here, but we upgraded you to a room at the Gran Hotel. Same rate, and we're sorry for troubling you."

With a sigh, Kayleigh relaxed. "Thank you. It's been a hard day and—" She stopped short. The woman didn't need Kayleigh's depressing life story. "Thank you so much."

"No, thank *you* for understanding."

"Okay." Kayleigh paused and then added, "Do you have the hotel's number? I'll need a shuttle."

"I can transfer you."

"That would be great."

Kayleigh waited a moment, and a man picked up the line. "Gran Hotel, this is Alejandro DeLeon. How can I help you?"

"I'd booked a room with City of the Crested Caracara Hotel. They said they transferred my reservation to you. Name is Kayleigh Kingston."

"Ohhh, yes, I took that call earlier today. Yes, ma'am. You're all set to check in when you get here."

Kayleigh breathed a sigh of relief. "Great. Do you have a shuttle or the name of a rental car company where I could get a vehicle?"

"No, ma'am. With the festival, everything is booked. We do have shuttles, and normally they'd run faster, but one of them broke down a little while ago.

We have one right now, and it's taking about an hour for new guests to get a ride."

"Okay, thank you. I'll go look for it and wait."

"Yes, ma'am."

She ended the call and leaned back on the bench, covering her eyes with her arm. At least she had a room. When she'd been booking hotels, she'd not been thrilled about staying at the City of the Crested Caracara place. It had looked…sketchy. At least something had worked in her favor for once. Still, the stress of the day was sitting heavy on her, and now she had to wait another hour to even get to the hotel.

"Kayleigh?"

Lifting her arm, she looked at Tru. "Hey."

He seemed to hesitate and then took a seat next to her. "I don't want to be pushy at all, but are you okay?"

As hard as she tried to keep her lip from trembling and the tears at bay, she couldn't. "No." A gush of tears poured down her cheeks. A better hotel wasn't going to get her or that artifact to New York. "I don't have a car, and there are no rentals available. I have to pick up that piece tomorrow and drive it back to New York, and I have no idea how I'm going to do it."

"Could you fly it instead?"

"No, it's too large. I asked London why it couldn't fly, but she said she didn't trust anyone but me. Me! And now

I've let her down, and I don't know how to fix it. I had a van reservation and everything." She wasn't always this whiny, but it just seemed like the world was out to get her.

Then her mouth went into overdrive. "I always manage to mess things up. Not just at this job, but everything. It's like I can't ever do anything right no matter how hard I try." The defeat settled into the pit of her stomach and stretched into her soul. Failed relationships. Failed jobs. Failed everything. It seemed *F* was stamped on every facet of her life.

Tru palmed her arm. Even as miserable as she felt, little tingles marched up her arm, almost making her squirm. For a moment, he seemed to study her. "My friend was supposed to meet me here, but he called just as I got off the plane to say he's not able to make it. I'll be on my own this trip, which means I'm free to do what I want. I could drive you."

What? She couldn't do that to him. "I need a large van, not just any vehicle. There's no way I could ask that of you. That's entirely too much."

"I don't want you to lose your job. If I can help, why wouldn't I?" He paused and then he gave her a half-grin. "It just so happens that a work van is what they rented me because it was all they had left with the festival going on. But you could have my rental, I guess."

"Absolutely not!" That was even worse than the

first option, even if she did wonder if they gave him her rental. She couldn't let him give up his rental for her. It wasn't right. But she did need it to keep her job. "That wouldn't be fair. It wasn't your fault my reservation got lost."

For a second, he seemed pained, but it was so quick that she pushed the thought away. More than likely, he just felt bad for her. His face lit up with a smile. "Then compromise. I can drive you and still get to sightsee. Were you driving all the way to New York City?"

Nodding, she said, "Yes, but my first stop is customs in Houston." If he went with her, she wouldn't be traveling through Mexico all by herself, which, if she were being honest, scared her to pieces. The only reason she'd agreed to it was because London kept mentioning how she needed someone to go.

"All right. I can take you there and then just drive back or fly back. No harm, no foul. I've got the vacation time."

She threw her arms around his neck, realizing the mistake as she inhaled his cologne. He looked good, smelled good, and he was kind and generous. If Prince Charming existed, he was Thaddeus Turner, and she'd never felt more like Cinderella in her life. "I'll never be able to thank you enough. Never."

His arms wrapped around her. "I don't know. This

is pretty good." His voice was husky as his jaw moved against her hair.

He wasn't wrong. It was great, in fact. So wonderful that it would be nothing to grow accustomed to, but she couldn't until she'd come through for London—and herself. A guy like Tru didn't want a ditz. He needed someone better than that.

Slowly, she untangled herself. "You've been so kind to me."

"I think if you see someone in trouble and you can help, you should," he said, holding her gaze. "What hotel are you staying at? I'm at the Gran."

Her sister was going to freak out. Her favorite movie was *Serendipity*, and Kayleigh was living her own version of it. "Me too."

With a grunt, he shook his head. "No way. I have to say this is the weirdest trip I've ever taken."

"Me too." She wasn't complaining, though. Maybe this was the universe telling her it was okay if she had a relationship now. That she didn't need to have things totally figured out before finding Mr. Right.

Then again, how many times had she fallen for a guy and been completely wrong about him? She'd followed Kip to New York City. He'd been sweet, fixing her broken guitar, tuning her piano...and then cheating her out of her music once he got her trust. She didn't want that to happen again.

No. Not this time. She had a goal, and a guy wasn't going to get in the way of it. This time she was thinking of herself first and keeping in mind that she wanted more out of life. She wanted respect, and she wanted her parents to look at her the way they looked at Autumn and Meesha. The only way to do that was to keep her job.

7

*A*s Tru walked to the van, he couldn't shake the feeling that the black-and-white assignment he'd taken in New York had turned pale gray. In an effort to get his thoughts in order, he'd offered to let Kayleigh wait for him at the terminal because she'd had a hard day and he could tell she was exhausted.

Before he'd approached her, he watched her a minute as she sat on the bench with his gut getting a full eight-minute ride as it bucked against what she'd been accused of doing. What he saw was a woman who was genuinely wrecked. He knew what that sort of defeat looked like. He'd experienced it right before leaving the military when he'd been confronted with his superior's corruption. It had shaken Tru to his core.

After turning eighteen, he'd joined the Marines and spent the next fifteen years serving. He'd been proud of his time in the military until he had a disagreement with his commanding officer. At the time, he didn't have the proof, but he was sure the man was stealing weapons and having them shipped back to the states. Of course, that left Tru with two options, staying to face discipline for false charges or retiring. He'd chosen the latter. It had weakened his faith in the system. Leaving the military and getting some counseling had helped him recover.

After working for a few security firms and butting heads with the bosses, he'd again found himself wandering. Until he'd been offered a job with the Guardian Group about seven months ago. So far, he'd enjoyed his time with them. Noah was a good man, fair and honest. Mia was great too. They'd had a few team members retire—men who still showed up from time to time to lend a hand—and it had been a pure blessing to Tru. At the time he was hired, he'd been a little lost.

When Tru reached the van he'd been assigned, he tossed his bag in the back before taking inventory of what Ryder had arranged for him. Mostly standard issue with some of it hidden in places that couldn't be easily seen just in case he needed it. He swiped the back of his arm across his forehead before getting into the driver's seat, rolling down the window, and flipping on the A/C. The air quickly turned cool, and there was a good chance it would at least be somewhat comfortable when he reached Kayleigh.

By the time Kayleigh came into view, he'd recommitted himself to following orders and sticking to his guns. But the smile she shot him as she spotted him took his commitment and his guns, tossing them out the window. The battle between his head and his heart was getting worse. They'd picked up swords and were poking him repeatedly.

Pulling to a stop, he put the van in park and hopped out.

"Was it that hot?" she asked, eyeing his sweat-soaked shirt.

"Like an oven. I sure hope the valet cracks the windows when he parks it." If they didn't, he'd assume they had a reason. Yeah, he'd taken out the rental insurance, but that didn't mean he wanted to use it if he didn't have to. He walked to the back of the van and pulled one of the doors open. "I got the insurance, so if something happens, it'll be taken care of."

"I was going to do that too. Better safe than sorry." She joined him, bringing her luggage with her. "Oh no, someone left their stuff in here," she said, spotting Ryder's supplies. "We should go tell the rental company."

As he sat the last piece of luggage down, he said, "It was a kit that came with the van, and since I was going to be traveling with my friend, I splurged. I don't think it'll hurt if we keep it." Good thing he was quick.

Kayleigh looked at Tru. "That's smart, and with my luck, maybe we should consider renting a second one." She laughed. "I'm sort of kidding. I think the statue will fit just fine."

"If not, we'll figure something out." He closed the door and walked Kayleigh to hers, pulling it open for her.

Her gaze caught his. "Thanks."

"My dad liked doing little things for my mom. It was his way of telling her he appreciated her. I guess it just rubbed off."

"I'm okay with that." The words were almost too soft to hear them over the noise of people arriving and leaving the airport. "I think it's sweet."

Instead of responding, he shut the door, jogged around the front of the van, and got in. Even if his gut was right, he had no future with her. Once she found out he'd been lying to her the whole time, she wouldn't give him the time of day. Especially after she confided in him about her ex.

"Okay, so, at lunch all we talked about was me, really. How about you tell me more about you? What made you decide to teach self-defense classes?" Kayleigh asked, angling toward him.

Again, this part of his cover wasn't made up. He

did teach self-defense through Guardian Group. It was one of the reasons he loved the company so much. They didn't want to just provide security; they wanted to teach people how to protect themselves too.

He glanced at her as he put the van in gear and pulled away from the terminal. "Self-defense is a skill everyone should possess. It keeps men, women, and children from being victims. Especially women and children. On average, they're abducted and kidnapped significantly more than men. I feel like I'm contributing something positive to my community and keeping it safer."

When she didn't respond, he glanced at her. Tears pooled in her eyes and twinkled in the sun. "So, beyond kind and generous, you're heroic too."

"It's not heroism to teach people how to protect themselves." He set his gaze back on the street and thought about all the people who had taken classes from him. "That show you talked about? Chuck? I looked it up on the plane. A regular guy making a difference in the world. That's what I like to do. You don't have to leap tall buildings to do that. It can be as simple as teaching a kid how to get away from a kidnapper. If I can keep one kid or one woman from becoming an abuse victim, it makes every class I've ever taught worth it."

"You may not think it's heroic, but it is. You devote

your time and energy to helping people. That's pretty stinking noble in my opinion."

He knew there would never be anything with her, but it made his heart happy that she appreciated his effort. "Uh, not sure how to respond to that."

"It's okay. Just means you're humble too."

Again, he didn't know what to say. The topic needed to move away from himself. "You said you have sisters?"

"Yep, Autumn and Meesha. One's a teacher and the other is in residency to be a doctor. I'm the oldest." There seemed to be sadness in her voice. He was sure there was a story there, but he wouldn't push.

"I have a huge family. Four brothers and two sisters. My mom and dad were both from big families too, so I have a lot of aunts, uncles, and cousins. Sometimes, it's easy comparing yourself to those who seem more successful." Understatement. His siblings were successful people who were able to balance their careers and families. Granted, they had their share of hard times, but it was easy to overlook when he was comparing himself.

She chuckled. "Yeah, I see your point. My family loves me; I'm not saying they don't. I want to hold myself to a higher standard. This will be the longest I've ever stayed at a job. When I interviewed for it, I thought there was no way I'd get hired. I was in this room with so many polished people, and when London called to tell me I got the job, I was floored. She'd been so intimidating. The first day on the job I was so happy, I hugged her." Kayleigh laughed. "It was beyond awkward. I shouldn't have done it, but I was so grateful."

"I bet she appreciated that you were excited to do the job. It's always easier to work with someone when you want to work for them." He paused as their hotel came into view. "Oh, wow, look at the architecture. The columns. This place is beautiful."

Kayleigh nodded. "Nicest hotel I've ever seen. Stunning. This is the kind of place where you wish the walls talked."

With a chuckle, Tru said, "Yeah, no kidding." He pulled the van to a stop at the valet station, got out, and went to the back to get their luggage, grabbing the firearms and hiding them in his bag as well. As he pulled the door open, a gentleman approached. Tru gave the man the key and registered with the service so they could pick it up in the morning.

She gasped as the doorman pushed the door open. "Look at those steps!"

His gaze rose and landed on a massive chandelier. "And that too." He pointed. During his flight, he'd looked up the hotel, but the pictures didn't express the grandeur of the building.

"Ohhhh, that is beautiful."

Tru set his hand on the small of her back as they took the steps. By now, he shouldn't have been feeling tingles, but they were just as strong as the first time. He quickly reminded himself of why he was in Mexico City and swept his gaze from side to side as they walked to the entrance. It was lined with flags and led to a five-story open lobby featuring an impressive atrium and caged birds.

It was the ceiling, though, that blew him away. Dazzling Tiffany stained glass took center stage and rocketed the lobby from amazing to speechless. They had obviously considered the architecture when they'd planned the seating, allowing tourists and guests to sit and take in the beauty of the place.

"This is breathtakingly beautiful," Kayleigh whispered.

She may as well have read his mind. He loved history and historical buildings, but this hotel was now his favorite.

Casting his gaze down, he locked eyes with Kayleigh. Okay, as far as beauty went, she won hands down. "It comes in second place." His voice was thick, and he loved the effect the compliment had on her. The way her cheeks turned pink and the sparkle in her eyes.

"I guess we should let them know we're here." She thumbed toward the check-in desk.

"Yeah, guess so."

They walked to the desk and were greeted by a desk clerk. "*Hola*, welcome to Gran Hotel." Her accent was thick, but Tru had experienced enough different cultures that he easily understood her.

"*Gracias, este hotel es hermoso. Me encanta la sensación del viejo mundo.*" Kayleigh rattled the words off so quickly that it took Tru a minute to translate them. He couldn't say he wasn't shocked. She'd thanked the woman for the greeting and told her the hotel was beautiful and she loved the old-world feel. "In one of the small towns I was in, there was a Hispanic farmer, and in exchange for milking the cows of a morning, he taught me Spanish. Well, almost. I had to leave before I knew much, but I continued it after I moved. It's such a pretty language."

The desk clerk seemed to appreciate that and beamed. "*Es un idioma bonito. Gracias, pero soy parcial.*" She laughed. "*¿Como puedo ayudarte?*"

"*Thaddeus Turner y Kayleigh Kingston, registrándose,*" Tru replied in Spanish, answering the desk clerk's question of how she could help them.

"You know Spanish too?" The way Kayleigh looked at him, she was as equally surprised as Tru had been.

"*Sí.* I just didn't want to speak a foreign language in case you didn't speak it."

Placing her hand on his arm, she leaned into him a little. "You really are a great guy."

She couldn't have punched him in the gut with a fist as hard as those words hit. Great guys didn't lie to women they could see themselves with, even if it had only been a day.

The thought slapped him. He'd known her all of a day. He needed to slow down and remember his promise to Noah. It was because of that promise that no matter how much he could see himself falling head over heels, the entire thing was based on a lie. That was no way to build a foundation for a long-term relationship.

They took care of the normal paperwork that came with staying in a hotel. As they did, the clerk told them about the restaurants and rooms. "We have a rooftop restaurant that overlooks the *Zócalo,* the main square where the festival will take place. The food is exquisite, and the view is romantic. There is also a bar located on the floor below the restaurant. We serve breakfast in the morning, or we also have room service should you want that instead." Tru had expected her to use Spanish once she knew they could speak it, but she was likely used to tourists who didn't speak the language and just spoke in English out of habit.

She finished processing the keycards and lifted her gaze to them. *"Está en la habitación trescientos cuatro,"* the clerk said, handing Kayleigh a key before giving him one. *"Y está usted en el trescientos dos."*

He was in room three hundred two, and Kayleigh was in room three hundred four. They were going to have a great view of the *Zócalo,* the main square in Mexico City. Man, Ryder had outdone himself with this hotel. For the rest of Tru's life, he'd be comparing other hotels to this one.

They thanked the desk clerk and headed for the old-world elevators that also sported stained glass. Tru ran his hand down one. "Wow. These have to be some of the first elevators in Mexico. I think this used to be a department store. If I'm remembering the website correctly."

"Really? That's so cool."

"I think it's been here since the middle 1800s."

"Wow," she replied as the elevator came to a stop and opened. She stepped inside, and Tru followed her. "London was the one who suggested that other hotel, but I'm glad they were overbooked now. I would have missed this."

He nodded. "Yeah, I hadn't realized how nice it was when I planned the trip. I just wanted to be somewhere central where I could walk some if I wanted."

When the elevator stopped on their floor, he

followed her out. Every time he looked around, a new detail would jump out at him. The intricate ironwork of the rails; the shape of the balconies; the way the stained-glass ceiling allowed light to filter through, casting colors everywhere.

They reached their rooms, and Kayleigh stopped at her door.

"Hey, you want to have dinner with me?" It had poured out so fast there was no way to stop it. They didn't have to eat together that night. He could have said he was tired or any other number of things, but she enjoyed the things he did. Being around her all day had made him realize how lonely he was and how much he wanted a relationship.

Her teeth caught her bottom lip as she nodded. "I'd really love that."

Well, he couldn't take it back now. If he were honest, it was more like he didn't want to. He looked at the time on his phone. "How about I knock on your door around seven?" It would give them two hours to clean up and get dressed, maybe even take a power nap.

"That would be perfect." She unlocked her door and slipped inside.

He entered his keycard into the reader and trudged into his room, setting his duffle bag down before walking to the bed. Flopping down, he scrubbed his face and groaned. What was he going to do?

He had orders, and they were sure they were correct. Still, the conflict between what he knew and what his gut said was raging so hard and heavy it had worn him out. *It had only been a day.*

Maybe having dinner would help. She'd slip up and say something to confirm her guilt, and it would be settled. At least, he could hope. Otherwise, he was going to crash and burn worse than he ever had before.

8

*L*eaning her back against the door, Kayleigh exhaled and slouched. Thaddeus Turner was the hottest man she'd ever met. He could speak Spanish, he loved history, and she could picture dates with him being filled with trying new things. She felt like Chuck Bartowski. If only Tru were a spy. She laughed aloud and pushed off the door. "Yeah, right."

If he were a spy, he would have been lying to her this whole time, and she wasn't sure how she would handle that. It would have to be a really good reason to do that, like saving the world or something.

She walked to the window and looked over the *Zócalo*. There were already a lot of people there, and when the festival started later, it would be packed. She sure hoped the room had good soundproofing. Otherwise, she wasn't going to get much sleep.

Then again, she was going to dinner with Tru. There was a very good chance thinking about him would keep her up all night. He hadn't called it a date, *per se*, but wasn't that what a date was? Going to dinner? By that logic, though, lunch had been a date too. She ran her hands down her face, flopped on the bed, and called her mom.

"Hey, KK," her mom answered. "You made it safely to Mexico City?"

"Yeah, I made it. I nearly peed my pants when the plane took off. When you and Dad said it was bumpy, you didn't say it would shake my liver loose."

Her mom snickered. "There really wasn't a way to prepare you for that. It shakes. I didn't think it was that bad."

Kayleigh snorted. "Maybe the tarmac was extra holey. I was next to this really attractive man. His name is Thaddeus Turner. I think for a moment I tried to sever his arm, I was holding on to it so tightly. Guess it worked out for me."

"An attractive man?" Her mom had that tone in her voice. The one she used with Kayleigh and her sisters when they talked about a guy. Her mom was so funny. She wasn't pushy at all, but she did remind Kayleigh of a meerkat. How they'd sit straight up and look around. Man? What man? Tell me about the man!

"Oh, Mom, he's just a guy. I just met him, anyway,

and he lives in Denver. Long-distance relationships—even if I was thinking about it—don't work. Besides, I've known him for less than a day." Should Kayleigh spill that she was having dinner with him? That he'd gone out of his way to help her? Maybe later would be a better idea. She didn't want her mom turning from a meerkat to a badger.

Her mom sighed. "All right. Fine. Thank you for calling and letting us know you got there safely. Don't forget to text your sisters too so they don't worry."

"Is that Kayleigh?" Her dad's voice was muffled slightly, like he wasn't all that close to the phone.

"Yeah, Trent, it's her. She got to Mexico City safely," her mom said. "She met someone too."

"Run, Kayleigh, run!" He spoke louder and laughed.

Her mom feigned a scoff. "Why, I never!" she said, the accent as Scarlet as her mom could get it.

Man, Kayleigh loved her parents. Their relationship was the gold standard for her. It's what she wanted when she finally met Mr. Right. "Okay, Mom. I think I'm going to go freshen up, take a short nap, and then walk around the city a little."

"Okay, sweetheart, have a good time."

They ended the call, and she quickly texted her sisters. Then she lay there a second, thinking how weird her day had been. How the plane hadn't been overbooked before she got on and then suddenly was. Her car reservation being lost, and then the upgrade to such a nice hotel. It was a string of circumstances that, when put together, created a plot no one would believe if they weren't experiencing it. Add Thaddeus Turner, and it went from unbelievable to fantasy.

---

*J*erking awake, Kayleigh grabbed her phone and checked the time. She hadn't even realized she'd dozed off. Now she had less than thirty minutes to get showered and dressed to meet Tru. She pushed off the bed and rushed to the bathroom, taking the fastest shower known to woman before throwing an outfit together. Just as she started to work on her hair, a knock came from the door.

Groaning, she blew out a puff of air as she looked at the wet cat staring back at her. Maybe this was good, though. Soaked hair, no makeup—not that she wore a ton, but still. No eyeliner, eyeshadow, or mascara made her look pale. If she looked horrible, it would kill any chance of things going somewhere.

She walked to the door and pulled it open.

The second Tru's gaze hit hers, he smiled. "You look great."

No, he looked great. Actually mouthwatering, wearing jeans and a t-shirt picturing the boom-box scene from *Say Anything* on the front. She loved that movie.

Kayleigh gave him a pointed look. "I look awful. My hair is wet—"

"It's pretty warm outside. It'll help you stay cooler." He grinned wider.

"No makeup..."

Shrugging, he said, "You don't need it."

Seriously? She needed him to be appalled. Horrified. Aghast, even. Instead, he was complimenting her. He needed to work with her on the whole no-relationship thing.

"Kayleigh, I didn't ask you to dinner because you're beautiful..." His eyes widened as he held up his hands. "But you are!"

She snickered. "Good save."

He laughed. "Whatever. I asked you to dinner because I enjoy your company. I think you are incredibly beautiful, but your personality and your quirks and your interest in the things I enjoy are what make you so attractive to me. A woman can be incredibly beautiful, but if it's only on the outside, it's just window dressing with nothing substantial to back it up."

Tru liked her quirks? "Does that include spilling coffee on you?"

He shoved his hands in his pockets. "If you hadn't, there's a chance I wouldn't have met you. I'm thinking that was worth a dozen coffee spills."

She threw her hands up. "Work with me here. I can't focus on keeping my job if you keep being perfect."

His smile died, and he caught her gaze. "I am so far from perfect. If…" He clamped his mouth shut. "Let's just say I have my quirks too. You just haven't seen them yet."

Kayleigh had no idea what quirks he could have, but so far he was wonderful enough that they could be overlooked. "You're sure you don't mind being seen with me?"

"I'll have the most beautiful, down-to-earth woman on my arm. I don't really care what anyone else thinks."

In that moment, she knew she was doomed. That path she was desperately clinging to had brought her to a fork, sidetracking her. The longer she stood there, the more enticing the diversion got.

"Okay." She turned, walked to the small side table, and grabbed her purse.

Holding his elbow out to her, Tru tipped his head

toward the elevator. "I thought we'd eat upstairs and then maybe go from there."

She slipped her arm through his and held on as they walked. He'd used the same cologne or after-shave, and he smelled amazing. She was lucky she remembered to put deodorant on. "I didn't mean to have a wet head. I called my mom to let her know I was safe, and I guess I dozed off."

"I crashed almost immediately." As they stepped onto the waiting elevator, he asked, "That's thoughtful to call your mom."

"My sisters and I usually call Mom and Dad on a regular basis. We're all pretty close." She leaned her head on his arm as the doors closed. "The only reason I've stayed in New York City is because of the gallery. I had decided the day that London called that if I didn't get the job, I was packing up my stuff and going home for a little while. I've missed them."

He covered her hand with his. "I totally get where you're coming from. The holidays are the best because I get to go home. I mean, I can go home more often than that, don't get me wrong, but Thanksgiving and Christmas are set in stone. Being in the military, I missed them for years, and I made a promise I wouldn't once I got out."

She lifted her head and met his gaze, appreciating the sweet gesture. "I missed this last Thanksgiving and

Christmas because London had me logging all the pieces that hadn't been done by the previous assistant. There were tons, and it was right after I'd accidentally taken her laptop. I didn't feel like I could say no."

The elevator came to a stop, and the doors opened. A heavenly aroma poured in, and Kayleigh's stomach screamed. "Sheesh. It's not like I didn't eat today."

"Yeah, but it smells amazing. I think I could be completely full and still want to chow down."

She laughed as they left the elevator and made their way to the host station. The man standing there greeted them with a warm smile. "*Hola*, two?"

"Reservations for Tru."

The man grinned wider. "Ah, yes, right this way."

Kayleigh looked at Tru as they followed the host. "You called in a reservation?"

He nodded. "I didn't want us waiting forever in case there was a crowd. The festival will be in full swing by the time we're done with dinner. I thought we'd go check it out."

"I'd love that."

They reached the table which was right next to the ledge where they could look out at the festival while they were eating.

"This is amazing," Kayleigh gushed, lifting on her toes to kiss Tru on the cheek.

His breath caught, and he blinked a couple of times

before covering the spot where she'd kissed him with his hand. "Yeah."

With the way he was looking at her, she got the feeling he wasn't talking about the view. She silently waved off the thought. He was just being nice.

He held her seat and then took his as the host placed the menus on the table. "Your waiter will be with you shortly." The man looked from Kayleigh to Tru before returning to his station.

They opened their menus, and by the end of the first page, she was salivating. Lamb, braised steak, and an assortment of pasta and sides. She zoned in on the desserts and tapped her chin, trying to decide if she wanted dessert first or to find the smallest entrée so she could make sure she saved room for one.

As he scanned the menu, he said, "I don't know what I want first, one of the entrees or to skip right to dessert. I'd need four stomachs, but I want to try it all."

A man after her own heart. "How about we get a few of the appetizers and a couple of desserts. I know they aren't entrees, but that way we can try as many as possible."

He nodded. "I like that idea. What sounds good to you?"

"Smoked scallops carpaccio?" She scanned the list of appetizers again. "Oh, or maybe the grilled marrowbone with garlic oil and epazote?"

"Both sound great. How about round it off with the artichoke fondue?"

"Sounds great to me." She looked up from the menu. "This is so much fun. I love doing this. I always have. Even my sisters and I do it. It's the best way to go out to eat."

He nodded. "Me too, but I come by it honestly. My parents did it when my siblings and I were growing up. It just became a thing."

Her jaw dropped. "Mine too!"

A waitress stopped at the table and clasped her hands in front of her. "Welcome to La Terraza. I'm Lucinda, and I'll be your waitress. Can I get you started with some drinks and maybe an appetizer?"

As far as fancy, this was the fanciest restaurant Kayleigh had ever eaten at. The only way she was affording it was because of London. Although, now that she was thinking about it, she wondered if her boss would be okay with her spending so much. If London had an issue, Kayleigh would just offer to cover the difference of what her boss would have found reasonable.

They gave Lucinda their drink and appetizer order. When they explained why, the woman seemed to agree that it was a great idea.

Kayleigh tucked a piece of hair behind her ear, thinking that maybe it was time she shared why she was so klutzy sometimes. "Uh, I do have something to confess."

His eyebrows knitted together, and he leaned forward with his arms on the table. "Okay."

"It's just…when I tell someone this, they look at me differently. Like I'm broken or something."

Instead of speaking, he just kept eye contact.

She swallowed hard. Getting the sad looks always bugged her. First, she parted her hair on the side. "This."

"What is that?" he asked just above a whisper.

"It's a scar. When I was twelve, I was helping my dad put up Christmas lights. I was on the roof at one end, and he was on the other. Something happened. I really can't remember what or why, but somehow, I fell. When I woke up, it was about a month later. I'd sustained a pretty serious brain injury."

"Okay."

"I had to relearn a lot. Like talking, walking, and other things. By the time I hit my twenties, the only lingering effect was getting overwhelmed when things were chaotic. I'll blackout sometimes. Not fall on the floor, but forget what I was doing and things like that. It won't be for long, but it happens." She quickly added, "But I've gotten a lot better. I started using these breathing techniques and counting and that stuff. It's helped a lot."

"I guess I'm looking at a miracle, then."

Her cheeks burned so badly she wanted to douse them in cold water. "I don't know about that, but I was lucky I lived."

"Have you had a blackout recently?"

"The last one I had was before I left for this trip, which was the first in almost a year. Somehow, I picked up the wrong laptop and I'm traveling with London's." She lowered her gaze to the table. "That's why I was so upset about the plane being overbooked. She said if I mess up this time, she's firing me."

Tru stretched his arm across the table and covered her hand with his. "Things have worked out, right?"

She lifted her gaze to his. "Yeah, but...I still have to make it back to New York City. It's only because of your generous offer that I even still have a chance at keeping my job."

"You'll make it, if I have to push the van myself." He pulled his hand back and winked.

Tears sprang to her eyes. "You've been so... wonderful to me. The last guy I dated was nice at first. Kip. He had these big dreams of becoming a singer. I was in Nebraska at the time. We'd find a huge field, sit outside at night, and watch the stars. We'd spend time together, play music. We were seeing each other about a month before he talked me into moving."

"Lucky for me." He winked.

So cute. "We were in New York for a few weeks before he started acting weird. A few more weeks passed, and I walked in on him with another girl, and they were doing drugs."

"What a loser." Tru laced the word with disgust.

"We had a huge fight. He...he hurt me. Not enough to go to the hospital, but enough that I wasn't staying in a relationship with him. I told him I didn't want to see him anymore. The next day, he used the key I'd given him to get into my apartment and steal all the songs I'd written."

"Okay, he was a double loser." Tru's eyes narrowed. "He better hope I never lay eyes on him. He *will* need a hospital."

She waved him off. "It's okay. It was last year, but he shook my confidence. I thought I could trust him, and I couldn't. How did I miss it?" One of the reasons she'd pledged to get her ducks in a row. Not only did she want a better professional life, but she wanted to have better relationships. If she felt worthy of more, she figured she'd attract better guys.

Guys like Tru.

9

*T*ru was buried in his thoughts as the waitress delivered their drinks and appetizers. It looked and smelled fantastic, and his stomach was in knots. He trusted Noah and knew the man to be honorable and thorough when it came to the cases the Guardian Group took.

In this instance, Kayleigh Kingston was not guilty. There was no way to convince Tru she was without hard proof—which they didn't really have. Unless there was a video or picture of her actually killing someone, his mind was made up.

This was no act. She was being completely genuine, and he knew it. Enough that he'd stake his entire job on it. Nowhere in the file did it list her having a head injury, but he'd seen the scar with his own eyes. Maybe she could have been lying about the cause, but that wouldn't make any sense. She had no reason to even show him. His gut was right from the get-go. Kayleigh was not who her file painted her to be, which made his lying even worse.

From the second she opened her hotel door, he knew he was falling for her. With wet hair and no makeup, simple jeans, and a t-shirt, she was exactly what he'd been looking for. Someone real and honest to walk through life with him. It had been mere hours, and it was completely illogical, but he knew. For now, though, he'd keep his word to Noah and maintain his cover.

"Oh, I don't know which one to start with first. They all look divine." The excitement in her voice pulled him out of his fog.

She was right. Everything looked great. The marrowbone sizzled, and the smell of the garlic was making his mouth water. "How about the fondue first so that bone doesn't nuke our tongues."

"Good idea."

They dug in and quietly ate a moment. "Thank you for telling me all that," Tru said as he finished his third bite.

Shrugging, she glanced up and back down at the table. "I know it's not a huge deal that there are a few lingering effects, but there are some, and sometimes they do affect me. But like I said, the last time was that laptop. Before then, it had been almost a year. The stress must have put a strain on me."

"Was that why you lost the painting?" Tru asked.

Kayleigh nodded. "Yes." It came out in a rush. "We had deliveries arriving, a few customers asking about certain paintings, and I was logging new items that had come in the day before. It was the next day when London informed me that I'd lost it."

Tru didn't let it show on his face, but he was beginning to have an alternate theory about Kayleigh's connection with London. Of course, there was no way to prove it without telling Kayleigh the entire truth, but with as much as she looked up to London, there was a good chance Kayleigh would call him a liar and side with her boss.

She'd called him perfect, and the brick-sized lump that formed in his throat had nearly choked him. Perfect wasn't lying to someone when he was near positive she wasn't guilty of what she'd been accused of. Then, like he needed a cherry on top of that compliment sundae, she'd kissed him on the cheek. If they hadn't been standing in the restaurant, he would have taken her in his arms and kissed her.

"Like I said earlier, you found it, so it all worked out." He popped another artichoke-fondue-soaked piece of bread into his mouth and ate it.

"I did, but it adds to the list of things I've bumbled

on." She inhaled and then let her breath out slowly. "Happier topic. What's your…favorite movie? There is a right answer." She laughed.

Kayleigh had the best laugh. It wasn't chirpy or high-pitched. It was soothing. One of the best things he'd learned about her so far.

He thought for a moment about the question. "It's going to sound totally lame, but I was having a sleep-over at my grandma's. I was flipping channels and landed on *The NeverEnding Story*, and I loved it. For years, I wanted to be Atreyu."

She gave a small snort, her eyes went wide, and she covered her nose with her hand. "You didn't hear that."

As hard as he tried, he couldn't hold back the laugh. "Hear what?"

"I will throw this bread at you." Her lips pinched together, trying to keep a smile from forming on her lips.

She had great lips too. Another reason he wanted to kiss her. He knew they had to be soft. "Was that movie the right answer?"

Lowering her hand, she said, "No, but you get a pass this time. The answer was *Die Hard*."

"I absolutely didn't see that coming."

"I love the action and being a hero." She ran her finger through some of the fondue on her plate and put it to her mouth. "I tried to join the military when I graduated, but my head injury prevented that."

Every detail she gave him only made him like her more. "I'm sorry. I bet you would've been great."

She looked around and leaned forward. "One of the ways I worked on my hand-eye coordination was by going to the gun range and shooting a BB gun because my dad went a lot. I'm not a perfect shot, but I'm not horrible."

Gun range. Whoever saw fit to put him on this case needed a good old-fashioned punch in the face. "I love going to the gun range. I wanted to keep up my skills after getting out of the military."

"You're probably a way better shot than me."

He grinned. "Actually, when I was a kid, I won a few local competitions in my hometown of Big Springs. A small town in Texas."

Sighing, she shook her head as he looked over the *Zócalo*. "I've never had so much in common with someone in my life."

"Can't say I have either." Which was the reason he was struggling so much. How could he have met the one woman he was looking for when he knew he'd wind up heartbroken and with her looking at him like he was a monster. He was lying to her. Not about who he was, but about why he was with her. Would she ever believe that he really liked her? Especially if she thought he believed she was capable of killing someone.

The waiter returned to the table and cleared the empty plates, handing them a dessert menu. They looked it over and eventually decided to go with three. Flan was listed, and there was no way they could come to Mexico and not try it.

When they finished with the desserts, Tru took care of the bill and they left the hotel to wander around the festival. It was packed with people and things to see. The entire time, he struggled to keep his mind from going down paths that weren't feasible.

Being with Kayleigh was fun. He'd felt more alive in the hours since that first flight than he had in years. Laughing about the same things, her stories about working with the farmer who taught her Spanish, and more than anything, she put his spirit at ease. He felt connected to her in a way he'd never felt before. The tightrope he was walking was shrinking, and the longer he was around her, the wobblier he got.

After a couple hours of wandering around, they found a food truck serving traditional Mexican desserts and ordered a few different ones to try, along with a couple of fruity drinks. They finished them and decided to relax a little bit before returning to the hotel.

"I'm so glad there's a breeze." Kayleigh pointed her

face into the wind. "I don't know why, but stuff like this seems more magical to me."

"Plus, you don't melt." Tru laughed.

"That too." She chuckled. "Do you mind telling me when you joined the military?"

He crossed his arms over his chest as he leaned back in his seat. "Right after I graduated high school. Most of my family have served at one time or another. My grandfather retired from the Marines, and so did my dad. Although, he teaches ROTC in my hometown, so he still works."

"Neat. My great-grandfather was in the Navy. He served something like forty years or so. A long time. He passed before I was born, but my mom tells me stories about him. From what she's told me, he was a good man."

"I don't know if I even considered doing anything else. From the time I can remember, I wanted to join. We went to airshows, military museums, and that kind of thing when I was growing up." He smiled. "How about you?"

"I grew up in Wyoming. My parents took us on quite a few long-distance drives. Most of the time there wasn't a plan, and we just bounced from place to place, checking out different things that interested us. I always thought it was fun. I left home a little after I graduated high school."

Loud music began pumping through the festival, and before they knew it, the courtyard was filled with people dancing the *Jarabe Tapatío,* also known as the Mexican Hat Dance. It lasted a little under two minutes, and that seemed to be an invitation to the crowd to join in on the fun.

Tru looked from Kayleigh to the crowd and back. Standing, he held out his hand to her. "Want to dance?"

Nodding, she took his hand. "Absolutely. Do you know that most guys don't want to dance?"

"My mom was a ballerina and dance instructor. I knew how to waltz by the time I was seven."

Her eyes lit up. "Really?"

Tru nodded. "Yep."

The music was lively, which seemed to energize both of them. After a few songs that had his heart pumping, the music slowed, and they even dimmed some of the lights. He put his arms around her waist and pulled her closer. "I think I'll sleep good tonight," Tru said.

Her hand came to rest on his chest. "Me too. That was fun, though. I bet you were very popular with the girls at school dances." The smile she shot him turned his brain to mush.

"Uh...kind of?"

She lifted a single eyebrow. "From the way your

cheeks are turning red, I'd say a little more than kind of."

He scratched the back of his neck. "It's..."

"You are so cute."

"I think you're amazing." He winked. He'd noticed when he did that, she'd giggle, and it seemed like she didn't even realize it.

Picking her up by the waist, he spun her around, and she laughed louder.

As he went to set her feet back on the ground, he paused, locking eyes with her. His gaze dipped to her lips. Those sweet, sweet lips had called to him all night. He'd never wanted to kiss someone as much as he wanted to kiss her.

"I...really like you. I feel...like..." She paused.

He knitted his eyebrows together. "What?"

She shrugged, setting her hands on his shoulders. "Like...maybe...my luck has turned around. You're pretty amazing yourself."

The spell was broken. He was a horrible man because he was lying to her. Would she understand why? Doubtful, and he wouldn't fault her. He could back off, though, so that when the truth came out, she wasn't too hurt. Which meant this little fantasy he was building needed to be shut down. Another relationship ended by his job, even before it could begin. Would he ever be able to have a family in this occupation?

Faking a yawn, he covered his mouth with his hand and set her down. "I'm so sorry. I think the day is catching up to me."

"Can't say I disagree. The last thing I need is to be late getting up tomorrow. London told me I had to be prompt."

"Let's finish this dance and call it a night."

She nodded and then laid her head on his chest.

If he didn't get a handle on his feelings, he was going to put this assignment in danger. He didn't want to let Noah down, and he didn't want to know there was a woman out in the world who hated his guts. How he was going to do both was becoming almost impossible.

10

"Thank you for breakfast," Kayleigh said, smiling. "Those pastries were so good." She leaned her back against her hotel door.

Instead of eating the hotel breakfast, they'd ventured out and found a small bakery with outdoor seating. She'd slept so little the night before, thinking about Tru. When she did finally manage to drift off, she'd dreamed about him.

Every minute spent with him had her wanting more. She loved his voice, his laughter, and the way he looked at her. Even after telling him about her accident, he hadn't treated her any differently. She'd gone a year without really mentioning it to anyone because she'd thought she was in the clear. It was only after her first mistake at the gallery that she became conscientious about it again. She didn't want to experience a blackout and be accused of deceit.

Tru's lips curved up, and their eyes locked. In an instant, she was alone in the world with him.

His smile faded, adding an intensity to his stare. He stood frozen in place, the crackling energy tightening the sphere, making it hard to breath. "They were, but I think it was the company."

Her heart galloped, racing at a speed that nearly made her breathless. She swallowed hard. "I have to agree."

He inched a little closer, braced his hand against her door, and leaned down. His eyes locked with hers, and it seemed like a storm was raging within him. Did he not want to kiss her? If it was anticipation he was trying to build, he was doing a fantastic job as he inched ever closer, leaving barely any distance between them.

One small shift, and her lips would touch his. If it were anything like she was anticipating, it would be the kiss to end all kisses. The kind she'd be using as a standard from that point on. Although, she had to admit there was a good section of her heart dismayed at the thought of kissing anyone else ever again.

His gaze dipped to her lips. "We barely know each other, but I feel a connection with you that I have never experienced before with anyone. I—"

With a single brush of his lips, there was nothing but him and her. Another sweep across hers, nipping at her bottom lip, and she circled her arms around his neck. The deliciously sweet kisses were tender, sending shockwaves throughout her body. Oh, she wanted more, more, more. *Forever.* The word tickled the edges of her thoughts.

Just as he was about to deepen the kiss, her phone sounded off, piercing through the bubble they'd created. She'd never wanted to smash something so badly in her life. Stupid phone.

Almost like he'd been slapped, Tru blinked. He quickly pulled back and straightened. "We probably need to get packed anyway. Don't want to be late. I'll see you in a few minutes." He grinned.

She pulled her phone out of her pant pocket. "It's London." It took work to keep her voice steady and the disappointment laced the words. Putting the phone to her ear, she let her door shut behind her. "Hi."

"I'm calling to let you know the pickup location has changed."

"Okay." Kayleigh debated whether to tell her about the van rental and the change in hotels.

London sighed. "You're keeping something from me. I can hear it in your voice."

Debate ended. "They didn't have a van for me when I got here, but—"

"I knew it. You can't be depended on. I don't even know why I trusted you to pick up this piece."

"I had a reservation. I showed it to you. How is this my fault?" Kayleigh didn't mind taking the blame for things she'd done, but holding her accountable for the rental company losing her reservation seemed wholly unfair. "Besides, I do have a way to pick up the piece."

For a second, her boss remained quiet. "Did you find another rental?"

"No, but a man I met on the way here—who, by the way, graciously gave me one of his seats on the first flight—has offered to drive me to pick it up and then take me to Houston."

"So, let me see if I have this right. You met a total stranger, someone you've never seen before in your life, and you put your trust in him to drive you to the pickup location and then take you to Houston? You have no idea who this man is. What if all he wants to do is steal it and ditch you in Mexico City?"

Shaking her head, Kayleigh walked to the bed and sat on the edge. "He wouldn't do that."

"And yet, here you are, with no vehicle and relying on someone you don't know. You didn't even think to contact me and give me a heads-up? Don't you think I should know if something goes wrong?"

"Yes, I do, but I thought you wanted me to take care of it. I'm trying, London. I showed you the reservation.

You know I had it." She paused. "Do *you* have anyone here who I could use instead of him? I'll thank him for the offer and tell him I have another ride."

"Yes, I do, but the reason I sent you was because they weren't available this time. I should have known better." London's tone dripped vinegar. "I guess I'll have to trust your judgment." She scoffed. "You don't leave that man alone for a second. Do you understand me? And he doesn't drive. You do. If this trip goes awry, you may as well stay home when you get back, because as of this moment, you are on notice. I like you, but I can no longer trust you."

The line went dead, and Kayleigh's hand drifted to her lap. If she could, she'd crawl back into bed and just cry the day away. One great smile, and all her focus had shifted to Tru. She didn't need a relationship; she needed to keep her job. If she had to start over some-where else...Her shoulders sagged at the mere thought.

Closing her eyes, she took a deep breath and let it out slowly through her nose. This wasn't how she was going to let things go down. She was capable of more than she gave herself credit for. If she had to get behind the van with Tru and push it to New York, she'd do it.

She stood and furiously packed her things while reciting affirmations to herself. This was just a bump in the road. Her obstacles were only in her mind. Even if something happened and she did fail, she was not giving up. She was going to make herself proud; she was going to put her life together. And one day, she'd find a remarkable man like Tru. When she was ready and not a day sooner.

As she stepped out of her room, Tru stepped out of his, and every affirmation she'd ever learned flitted from her mind. This man wasn't common. He was a rare find.

"Are you okay?" he asked.

Again, she steeled herself to finish the job London gave her. "I'm okay, but I'll need to drive. My boss called while I was packing, and she wasn't too thrilled that a stranger was going with me. I told her she didn't have to be. I trust you, but I'm desperate to keep my job. Would it be okay if I drove? If not, I'll have to find another way. I don't know how, but I will."

When he didn't speak, she sighed. "It's really okay. I appreciate everything—"

"No, I was just wondering if I need to call the rental company and add a driver. I'm fine if you drive. I can understand your boss's reluctance to trust someone she hasn't even met." He shrugged.

Kayleigh let go of her luggage, stepped forward, and hugged him around the waist. "Thank you so much for everything you've done for me. You've been so wonderful." She left out the part where she wondered what she'd do without him. What little time she'd spent with him had her thinking it would be winter in the middle of summer if he weren't around.

Tru wrapped his huge arms around her. "I believe I got the better end of the deal. I don't really care where I'm going as long as I get to spend time with you."

She leaned back. "I feel the same way."

What she wouldn't say was that those feelings were stronger than anything she'd ever felt before. Tru was gentle, and she felt safe when she was around him. No one had ever really given her that. Not even Kip. As much as she thought she loved him at the time, what was blooming in her heart for Tru was a full-on bouquet.

Stepping back, Tru said, "Let's get checked out and get on the road. Maybe if we're early, it will look good to your boss."

With a sigh, she said, "Okay." Her phone dinged, and she looked at it and back to Tru. "Directions. The location has changed. We're going straight east, it looks like. I guess that's good since it gets us closer to Houston."

"All right." He took a step and snapped his fingers. "I almost forgot my phone charger on the nightstand. I'm usually pretty good about remembering things, but...I was restless last night. I think I may need a little more coffee before we get on the road to Houston."

"I'll wait here for you. Keep an eye on our luggage."

"Thanks," he replied and slipped back into his room.

She nearly squealed with delight the second he left her sight. He didn't sleep well either. Had he thought about her as much as she'd thought about him? Was it possible she'd found her Mr. Right?

With a huff, she pinched the bridge of her nose. Inwardly, she chastised herself. They'd just met. She barely knew him. Even if she didn't already have a goal, it was too soon. This time she wasn't going to be so hasty. She needed to take a deep breath, slow down, and take her time. The journey was just as important as the destination. If she had to, she'd buy a permanent marker and write that on her arm. This time she was doing things the right way.

11

*A*fter nearly kissing Kayleigh the night before, Tru had come back to his room and chastised himself until he drifted to sleep. It had been fitful. Dreams about her were nonstop. He'd made an extra effort to remind himself that none of this was real and he had a job to do, but it seemed neither his head nor his heart was listening. Clearly, the scolding didn't stick because at the next opportunity, he'd kissed her.

He'd kissed her. He was disgusted with himself.

When he returned to his room while she took London's call, he'd walked straight to the bathroom and splashed his face with cold water. Holding her felt right and natural. Like she'd been crafted just for him. What he was doing was all sorts of wrong.

What did that say about his character? She was sweet and trusting, and he'd done something he couldn't take back. This thing with Kayleigh was getting dangerously close to breaking his heart. He wasn't deliberately leading her on. His mouth was running so fast his brain couldn't catch up.

Now, he sat on the edge of the bed and dialed Ryder. The location pickup had changed, and the team would need to know. The line picked up, and Tru said, "Hey."

"Hey," Ryder answered. "What's up?"

"Two things. First, she's got London's laptop."

"What?" Tru could almost see the man sitting on the edge of his seat. "If we can get our hands on that laptop before anyone can wipe it, it could be a gold-mine of information."

Tru was good with a computer, but Ryder and Mia were masters. Those guys had cracked some of the toughest encrypted information he'd ever seen. Maybe that laptop would also prove Kayleigh's innocence. "Should I try to grab it?"

He seemed to debate a moment. "If you can without spooking her, yeah. If there's even a question, don't. We're still trying to weed out the mole. What's the second thing?"

"Location change. It's straight east now. Once I get to the van, I'll turn on the tracking device so you can keep tabs on our location. If I manage to get a second to send the actual address, I will."

"Okay. Anything else?"

"I'm still not convinced she's guilty. I've got a theory, but I want to flesh it out a little more before I say anything."

Ryder sighed heavily. "Tru, look, I get it. Getting close to someone is hard, but you have to stick to the plan. If we're right, she could turn on you in a second. Who's to say she wouldn't kill you too? We have reliable information that she is exactly who we're telling you she is."

"But—"

"No, Tru." Ryder's fierce tone sent Tru's hackles up.

"I'm the one who had dinner with her last night. I'm the one who danced with her. Looked her in the eyes—" He cut the sentence short, getting his temper under control before confessing he'd kissed her. "She's not guilty because she couldn't hurt a fly."

Ryder groaned. "You aren't supposed to be dating her. You're just supposed to stick close. I don't want to be a jerk here, but do you need to be pulled from this case? If so, we can just let the local police take her and see if we can get her to cooperate and turn on London."

Kayleigh stuck in a Mexico City jail? Tru's heart hit the floor. He couldn't do that to her. He hated lying, but if being fully transparent led to her being thrown in jail in a foreign country, he'd resign himself to keeping his cover. "No, I'm fine. I'll get the artifact, get her to Houston, and let it shake out there."

"Are you sure? Seriously, Tru, I know it can be hard, but there's a reason why we do things the way we do. Noah's the boss. We either listen or leave."

Nodding, Tru stood. "Yeah, I know. Let me go. We need to get on the road so we aren't late."

"Get your head clear and stick with the plan. We'll see you in Houston."

"Yeah, man." Tru rubbed his hand over his hair. "Talk to you later."

He ended the call, and when he reached the door, he leaned his forehead against it. Ryder was right. All Tru had at the moment was what his heart and his gut were telling him. Ryder had actual documentation. If he were wrong, he could blow the whole mission. When he said he'd follow Noah's orders, Tru had meant it. Until now, it had been easy, and he wasn't the type of man to back away when things were tough.

With his thoughts in order, he straightened and stepped out of the room, plastering on a smile that he hoped hid the confusion he felt. "Ready?"

Kayleigh's lips quirked up. "Find your charger?"

"I guess I packed it. I don't remember sticking it in my suitcase. Maybe I was a little too distracted as I was getting my stuff together." He winked as he hinted about the kiss they'd shared.

She cut him a glance. "Right."

Once they'd returned their room cards, they requested their van and got on the road. The built-in navigation was nice because she typed in the address, which allowed him to pass the information on to Ryder.

"Thanks again for letting me drive."

"It just means I get to nap while we're on the road." He laughed.

She huffed. "What? You have to stay awake so you can keep *me* awake."

He covered his mouth as he yawned. "We're going to need to stop for some coffee if that's the case."

"Don't yawn. That stuff is—" She yawned and shook her head. "Catching. Whew. Yeah, we're going to need coffee. Lots and lots of coffee."

He cleared his throat. "Uh…"

"Go ahead and ask me anything you want about it." She quickly looked at him and back to the road. "You want to ask me about my injury."

"How on earth did you know that?" Was he that transparent? Mostly, he wanted information for the theory he was working on.

She shrugged. "Your tone. I just knew. I've lived with the questions all my life."

He twisted in the seat to face her. "You don't have seizures?"

"If I did, I wouldn't be driving, so no. Actually, according to my doctor, I'm cleared."

Cleared? "But you still have blackouts?"

"That was a quirk from when I was younger. I think the head injury just amplified it. I was never great in crowds or hectic situations. For a while, my parents thought I had autism, but testing proved I didn't." She shot him a small grin.

"Did you have yourself checked again after you started working for London? When the mistakes started happening?"

Shaking her head, she replied, "No, most of the reason I tell people about the head injury is because it was a big life-altering moment. That's not something you leave out when you like someone." She rolled her lips in. "I mean…"

"It's okay. I…I like you too." He faced the front again, forcing himself to focus on his line of questioning. "Does London know about it?"

"Oh, yes. On the application, it asked if I had any medical issues she needed to be aware of, and I told her about it."

Tru crossed his arms over his chest. The application in her file didn't show that. "And you only started blacking out again when you started working for her?" he asked and then quickly added, "I mean, I suspect the stress of wanting to do a good job could cause one, right?" He didn't think that to be true at all. What he was beginning to suspect was that Kayleigh was being set up, including the file Guardian Group had been given on her.

She pressed her back into the seat and seemed to get a little more comfortable driving in the Mexico City traffic. "Honestly, at first, I wasn't really all that stressed. Just excited because it was such a neat opportunity. The first gallery showing we had was for Julian Wolf. His stuff was amazing. There was so much soul in his work. He was a really nice man too. So down to earth. I never got the feeling that he was snobby. His wife was sweet too."

"Julian Wolf?" Noah's brother? How wild was that? "I've heard of him."

"About two months after I started working there, we got this rush of new talent coming in. Of course, that would happen after one of the staff quit. I never met the employee because he worked overnight logging arrivals."

"That was the reason you couldn't go home at the holidays, right?"

"Yep. Come to find out, the jerk hadn't been doing his job for months. London was so furious. After that, it was just me. I guess she didn't trust anyone enough to hire someone else." Kayleigh looked at the navigation. "This next turn is our last. It sure seems out of the way, doesn't it?"

Tru looked around. "Yeah, it does."

"Maybe they store things out here so tourists or thieves can't find them." She slowed the van. "Some of these buildings look kind of creepy."

Most were so dilapidated that only shells remained. The road curved, and ahead in the distance stood a place that didn't look like a place to keep priceless antiques. Nothing about it looked secure at all. "Are you sure this is the right place?"

She grabbed her phone from the dash. "Yeah, see." She held the phone up for him.

Two Caucasian men stepped out of the front door and waved them forward. "They don't look like people from a museum." Tru swept his gaze from one side of the home to the other. A weird feeling pooled in his gut. He knew they were meeting black-market dealers, but something about this wasn't right.

Kayleigh tapped a number on her phone and put it to her ear.

"If you're calling to tell me you didn't—" Tru could hear the older woman loud and clear.

"I'm here, but I wanted to double-check with you. Is this rundown place really where I'm supposed to meet them?" Kayleigh asked and then told her the address showing on the navigation. "This is correct?"

"Yes…it may not look like much, but the museum is in the process of restoring. Let's just say appearances may be deceiving."

"All right. Well, I'm here and"—as Kayleigh replied, she looked up—"they're motioning for me to turn the van around. I'll make sure to send you a picture once it's loaded."

"Good. You may end up keeping your job after all. I'll see you in New York."

"O—" Kayleigh hung up. "I get I've messed up in the past, but the car rental thing wasn't my fault. I had a reservation." Her shoulders rounded as she hung her head. "I guess she's just sick of me."

"I'm sure it'll all work out." That wasn't technically a lie. It was just not going to end up like she thought.

A man tapped on the glass, and Kayleigh rolled the window down. "Hi, I'm here to pick up a large…" She tapped a few times on her phone. "This. I don't want to butcher the name, and I'm sure I'd do that."

The man smiled. "We'll load it quickly so you can be on your way." The man's eyes seemed to roam over her face, not in an appreciating way, but like a predator. "You are very beautiful. Are you staying in Mexico City overnight?"

She must have felt the same thing as Tru because she leaned away from the window. "Uh."

"No, and if she were, she's with me." Tru leaned over, kissing her cheek.

Grabbing Tru's hand, she tangled her fingers in his. "Yep, my guy here was kind enough to take off work and help me."

Flicking his gaze from Kayleigh to Tru, the man's eyes narrowed a fraction and stepped back. "Lucky man. I'll go get your statue loaded."

"Thank you."

She quickly rolled up the window. "Those men are not from Mexico."

He knew that, but he was surprised she did. "How do you know that?"

"You didn't hear the slight African accent? They were trying to sound native, but they weren't."

"Just how many spy movies have you watched?"

With a giggle, she said, "A lot. Plus, I love language. I love how people speak. It's interesting to me."

She was amazing. He'd barely picked up on that accent, and he had way more experience than her. Unless his gut was wrong and she'd done this a few times.

Before he could respond, the back doors to the van were pulled open and a forklift came from behind the house carrying a statue. "For some reason, I pictured it bigger."

"I was under the same impression. This absolutely

could have been shipped." Her eyebrows knitted together, and she looked at Tru. "We did have a piece—"

The men loading the statue began to talk in Spanish, and Kayleigh stopped midsentence and froze. Tru understood what they were saying too, and they weren't gentlemen speaking.

Leaning in, she whispered, "I should give them a good piece of my mind."

Tru grabbed her arm. "Don't." He'd tell her who they were and about their concealed weapons once they were on the road. "Trust me."

Her eyes locked with his, and she nodded.

As soon as that statue was loaded, they were going to blaze out of there while he texted Ryder to tell him the men at the pickup location were armed ex-prisoners and Number's gang members, an African prison gang with a reputation of being deadly. He'd dealt with them in a case prior to joining Guardian Group while he was working for a security team in London. This case was taking a direction none of them could have predicted. Hopefully, the whole thing wouldn't blow up in their faces.

12

Kayleigh's plan to drive up the coast of Mexico after picking up the statue was nixed when Tru advised her that it wasn't a good idea. Entering Texas through Laredo was much safer, unfortunately. It saddened her because she loved the beach. She'd had visions of walking along the shore, holding hands with him, and perhaps, maybe, another kiss. This time, she'd make sure her phone was turned off.

Now that they were pointed in the direction of Laredo, she settled into the driver's seat and looked at him. "So, why didn't you want me telling them that was no way to talk about a woman?" Ohhh, she'd been so mad. They were saying horrible, ugly things about what they wanted to do to her, thinking she couldn't understand the language. The way Tru had looked at her, though, she knew she needed to listen. Now, she was even more grateful she'd run into him. He'd probably saved her life just then.

"They were wearing guns. I could see the outline of them." He folded his arms over his chest, pinning his gaze to the floorboard with a grim expression. "And by the looks of their tattoos, they were members of an African prison gang called Numbers."

"Maybe the museum director hired them." She assumed so, anyway, since the director was the one lending the statue to Beacon.

He twisted in his seat. "Kayleigh, have you looked into London at all?"

"No, I've had no need to. She's been a pillar in the art community for three decades. I've seen the awards and accolades. She's very opinionated and passionate, but that doesn't mean anything." London was well-known. If an artist wanted to break out, they came to her.

Tru rubbed his knuckles along his jaw. "Just because she has all that doesn't mean she's not questionable. It just means she hasn't been caught."

She scoffed. "London is a great boss."

"Who has treated you pretty horribly since this trip started."

Okay, so he had a point, but he had no idea what it was like putting up with all the klutzy stuff Kayleigh did. "She has a right to be that way. There have been many times she could have fired me and didn't. This was just her last straw."

"I'm just…didn't that seem odd to you?"

"I guess, but I've never done this before. I don't know what this sort of thing is supposed to look like. All I know is that London Carter is the first person to ever not toss me aside because I was inconvenient."

"Did you have a job before you followed Kip to New York?"

"I did, but I'd only had it about four months before I left. Part of what has bothered me so much is that I gave up everything for a guy who turned out to be nothing but a jerk. That's why I'm trying to hold on to this one so much, because I'm tired of seeing myself as a failure." The words tumbled out of her mouth so fast and furiously that she couldn't hold them back. "I want to be more than a flakey girl who follows her heart and any guy that pricks my interest. It's one of the reasons I promised myself that I'd put relationships on hold until I was able to get my feet on solid ground and keep them there."

The silence had stretched to an almost uncomfortable level when Tru replied, "Oh." It was soft enough that she nearly didn't catch it. "That's…that's a good goal. You should do what makes you happy and fulfilled."

That wasn't how she'd meant it all to come out, but

maybe it was best this way. If he thought she wasn't interested, maybe...maybe he wouldn't act interested either. They could get to Houston, and she'd be just as single as when she left New York. "I think it will."

Twisting in his seat, he laid his head against the headrest and looked out the passenger window. How did he make something so simple seem so...heartbreaking?

Kayleigh wanted to cry. Hadn't she said that morning that he was a once-in-a-lifetime sort of man? So far, he'd treated her with nothing but respect and kindness, and she'd just repaid him by biting his head off. And for what? Her boss? The same woman Kayleigh questioned just minutes before. Now she couldn't decide if she was a hypocrite or just flakey.

At the first gas station, she pulled in and parked at a pump. "I thought I should fill up just in case. Plus, I thought it would be a good break."

Tru unbuckled his seatbelt, opened the door, and paused. "Do you want to go in first or me?"

"You can go ahead. I'll start filling it up."

"Okay, see you in a minute." He smiled, but it didn't even come close to the ones he'd given her before her little rant.

The moment he was out of earshot, she leaned her head against the steering wheel and groaned. She didn't need to make a choice. She was both. A flakey hypocrite. Getting out of the van, she grabbed her wallet, walked to the pump, and began fueling up.

Why had she defended London so vigorously? During Kayleigh's interview, she'd been almost harsh. To the point where Kayleigh almost hoped she didn't get the job. But then when London had called, it seemed like she was another person. Kayleigh had given her the benefit of the doubt because hiring an employee was stressful. What was the excuse for all the other times when London was overbearing? Even in situations when Kayleigh hadn't been at fault, London had treated her not-so-great. Missing Christmas was just one of many examples.

Kayleigh set the toggle on the pump and leaned her back against the van, chewing her thumb as she thought about her time at the gallery. She'd given London several passes that had her questioning why. Yes, Kayleigh had made mistakes, but she'd also fixed them. Most of the time while London raged about how incompetent Kayleigh was.

"In deep thought?" Tru's voice broke through the thoughts racing around her head. He held up a cooler. "Got us some water for the road. I thought it might be a good thing so we don't have to stop so often."

She straightened as he reached the back door and pulled it open, setting the cooler next to the statue. "That was a really good idea."

He opened the cooler and started ripping the bag of ice open. "I figured if we needed more, I'd go back. I only had so many hands, and it wasn't exactly—"

Taking his face in her hands, she cut him off by kissing his cheek. "Thank you, and I'm sorry for biting your head off about London. You were sticking up for me, and I just rolled right over you."

Blinking, he slowly nodded. "It's okay. You have a right to want to live your life how you want to. I just… those guys weren't on the up-and-up to me. I'm not saying you can't take care of yourself, but there were more of them than you, and they were armed. London should have given you a heads-up or used a more ethical acquisitions company."

"I know." What had Kayleigh done to deserve a guy like Tru? "I'm going to run in and grab snacks. I think that's enough ice."

"Okay. I'll have us ready to go by the time you get back."

As she got to the entrance to the store, Kayleigh looked over her shoulder. Like the night before, Tru had his hand on his cheek. Like he was cherishing it. To her, that was one of the most romantic moves a man could make, and he was doing it in reaction to her. Giddiness bubbled from her core, and she could barely contain the excitement. She couldn't remember a guy doing that with one of her kisses.

After she'd amassed a range of snacks, she paid and went back to the van. "I think this should do us," she said, handing the bag full of goodies to Tru.

He pulled it open and laughed. "Did you buy the whole store?"

"No, but I have no idea what might be available on this road, and this was a sure thing. I got candy, chips, and some protein so we're not waddling out of this van by the time we reach Houston."

"Uh, even with the protein, that's a good possibility." He chuckled. "Oh, man, I love these things," he said, pulling out a Payday candy bar. "I could eat my weight in them when I was a teenager. I don't think I ever went anywhere without one."

She buckled her seatbelt and cranked the engine. "And the list of things we have in common just keeps getting longer."

He looked at her. "Really?"

"Yes. I love them. I figured whatever I had leftover I could eat when I got home." Back on the road, she glanced at him. "I really am sorry I bit your head off. London was nice to me at first, and now I feel like I'm required to stick up for her."

"It's okay. We've known each other a day, so the peanut gallery can just stop talking." He grinned.

She nearly sighed in relief. His amazing smile was back, and she didn't want to see it vanish ever again.

He didn't seem to care about her injury, the blackouts, or any of her quirks. Long-distance relationships were hard, but not impossible.

Why couldn't she have him and her job? She could multitask. Besides, long distance could be the best solution. There would be designated times when she'd get to see him, and on the other days, she'd give her full attention to the gallery.

It was a win-win. Right?

Inwardly, she groaned. Why couldn't she just keep her focus on herself? Every time she promised herself she'd keep her feet on the ground, she'd go find a hot air balloon and off she'd go again. When was she going to learn?

A relationship was a relationship, long-distance or not. It took work and time spent together. What if London gave her more work like this past Christmas? Would Tru stick around? Maybe, but would it be fair?

Why was she even thinking about this in the first place? Again, her heart was putting the cart before the horse. She needed to slow down before she found herself out of control. If it was meant to be, they'd meet again when she was in a better position to be someone's girlfriend.

13

*T*ru wasn't just flirting with danger anymore; he was actively participating in it. He chastised himself about going any deeper, but every time she touched him, he wanted more. She'd apologized for getting upset and then kissed his cheek. The spot was still sending zaps into his gut.

His phone buzzed in his pocket, and he pulled it out. "Sorry, work."

"I've got no room to complain."

Have you had any chance at all to look at the computer? Ryder asked.

Tru cut a glance at Kayleigh. *Yeah, while she was in the convenience store. Password protected. I would have called, but I didn't think you'd have time to break into it. I also didn't want to get caught.* He didn't want to be stranded in Mexico, and he didn't want her driving alone either.

Yeah, with us this close, we don't need anything going wrong.

Have you had any luck with the mole? Tru asked.

Not yet. Maybe if we can get into that laptop, we can find out who it is.

Maybe it would prove Kayleigh is innocent too. He typed it out and went to delete it but hit send instead. Did his brain have any connection with the rest of his body anymore, or had it gone completely rogue?

And that would be great for her if it does. For now, our job is to get her, the laptop, and that artifact to Houston so we can put the picture together. If she's innocent, I'll be the first to apologize.

Did the police grab the guys at the pickup? Was I right? Were they Numbers?

Yeah, we got them. We don't know anything beyond that yet.

Tru frowned.

"Bad news?"

He looked up from his phone. "What?"

"You were frowning. I thought it might be because of bad news or something."

"Oh, no, everything's fine. I was just deep in thought." Maybe.

Another text came through from Ryder. *Police gave us a warning, though. That wasn't all of them.*

How do they know?

They've been picked up before and released almost immediately. Once it's out that they were arrested, it might get ugly. Keep your heads down and get across the border as quickly as you can.

Will do.

Tru pocketed the phone again and set his ankle over his knee. "So, tell me more about your sisters." Maybe he could glean something from that. Something to help give him a cease-fire from the raging war going on between his head and heart. "Autumn is the youngest and in residency, right? And Meesha is a teacher? Has she been in Paris long?"

Nodding, she replied, "Yeah, Autumn is in her last year. She was always wanting to play doctor. It was her calling." She sighed. "And Meesha has been in France a little more than a year. A few weeks ago, she put in her two-week notice, and she's moving back home." Kayleigh's lips pinched together.

That wasn't the face of someone who had a close relationship with her sister. "Are you upset by that?"

"Yeah, because she's not doing it voluntarily. She's getting away from an abusive ex-boyfriend." Kayleigh looked at Tru. "I'm so worried about her. I'm the only one she's told because she's embarrassed. I promised I'd let her tell our parents and Autumn."

"There is no reason to be embarrassed. Have the police stepped in? Does she have a restraining order?" The questions came out quickfire.

Kayleigh glanced at him. "I can definitely tell you teach self-defense. Maybe you could show me a few moves and I could show her sometime."

Tru grumbled a few unkind words under his breath. "I hate that. A victim isn't the one who needs to be embarrassed. It's the perpetrator who should be. They take a person's confidence, safety, and peace."

"Well, Meesha is shaken. He's been put on a no-fly list, so she's coming back to the States so she doesn't have to live in fear."

With a good lawyer, that individual would probably be out on the street in no time, and there was no telling about his traveling abilities.

"I don't want to be the bearer of bad news, but that's easier said than done. She still needs to be vigilant. She'll need some solid support and a counselor, even if she isn't showing signs of stress. It can hit without warning and take your breath away." If Kayleigh didn't despise him when this was all over, he'd offer to teach Meesha some self-defense.

Kayleigh touched his knee. "Thank you. I'll tell

her." She chewed her lip a moment. "You seem to know what you're talking about with the counselor."

"Uh, yeah, working with victims. Even the strongest need someone to talk to." He paused, wondering if he should confide in her about his experience, and quickly decided against it. Intimate details about himself would give her even more reason to hate him later on. Even if he spoke from the heart, she'd never believe it.

"I can't imagine. It must be hard sometimes."

He pinned his gaze on the radio. "It doesn't compare to what the victims have been through. What kills are the ones who don't make it. Either by the person who was threatening them or..." His voice broke. Since working with the Guardian Group, they'd only lost two victims, but it was two too many. "I know it's not my fault, but I take them hard."

"Because you're a good guy."

The soft-spoken words should have been a balm, but it only made him feel worse. How was Kayleigh going to feel when she found everything out? It wouldn't matter if she was innocent; she'd hate him either way.

Hopefully, it wouldn't last forever. Maybe she'd understand why and be okay. If he got nothing but friendship, it was better than nothing. The sentiment sounded nice, but his heart broke at the thought.

"What about your family?" she asked.

Should he tell her about them? What if Noah was right and his gut was wrong? "Uh, I'm smack in the middle. My four brothers are older than me, and my two sisters are younger."

"You made their dating lives miserable, didn't you?" She shot him a smile.

He laughed. "Actually, no. Most of the time we tried to be friends with them. That way they didn't feel threatened and our sisters trusted us if something went wrong." He crossed his arms over his chest. "My sister, the one born after me, had a guy skirt the line once. She came to us—well, the whole family—and told us. We nipped that problem in the bud. My oldest brother—who's bigger than me, by the way—was a Marine as well. He actually made the guy pee his pants. Needless to say, that guy straightened up."

Kayleigh looked at him, eyes wide. "Bigger than you? Are you related to King Kong?"

He tipped his head back, laughing harder than he had in a long time. "No, but it does seem that way. So far, I've avoided beating my chest or stealing damsels."

"You know, you're really nothing like I expected. Just when I think you'll fit in a mold, you break it." She glanced at him. "I think that's what I like most about you."

"I could say the same about you."

"Not really." She shook her head. "I'm a ditzy klutz who talks too much and—"

"Stop," he said. "You aren't ditzy. Not even close. You knew those men weren't native to Mexico. And everyone is clumsy at times. I like that you talk too much. I especially like it when you blush. When you wrinkle your nose or laugh. You enjoy the things I do. I like you just the way you are."

She swiped at her eyes with her hand. "Other than my family, you're the only person who has ever said something like that to me."

"You've been spending time with the wrong people, then. Your quirks are what...draws me to you." With iron chains. His heart had taken over his mouth and spilled out words he wouldn't take back.

"Thank you." She spoke so softly he almost didn't hear her. Clearing her throat, she said, "Okay, we've talked movies, food, and a little about family. What about music?"

He grunted. "Classical. I especially love acoustic guitar."

"I don't have a favorite. I love it all, and I have since I was tiny."

"You said your ex stole your songs. Even though he took them, does that mean he can get away with it? I thought there were copyright protections."

Nodding, she replied, "There are, and I can prove I

had them long before he took them. If he didn't sound like a bellowing whale, I might be worried a little. His voice was not what made me fall for him." She tilted her head as she looked ahead. "Honestly, I can't even remember why I liked him at all."

Tru shifted in his seat. "I've had a few of those, but I think I was trying to shove a square peg into a round hole. I wanted the feeling of connection and love so badly that I was blind."

"Yeah…"

The women he'd dated were okay. There wasn't anything he could point to that made them the wrong fit; they just weren't…he really didn't have a word for it. All he could do was compare them to how he felt with Kayleigh. It had been instant. This feeling of finding his other half. A sense of belonging to someone that he'd never experienced before.

And all of it was for nothing, even if he was ready to leave his job to be with her. Because there was only one ending he could see, and it was fully engulfed with fire. A plummet to earth so hard and fast that there would be a crater where his heart used to be.

14

Sitting back, Kayleigh groaned. "I think I broke my stomach."

Tru's head fell back as he laughed. "It hurts, but totally worth it."

She laid her head back on the bench seat and rolled it to look out the window. "There's a cute little shop over there we could check out. Maybe walk a little of this meal off."

"I'd get favored-uncle status if I brought a few things home." He sighed. "That's if I can move. Either I was hungrier than I've ever been before or that's without a doubt the best food I've ever had."

"It could be both." The small hole-in-the-wall restaurant they'd happened upon in Tula De Allende, about an hour and a half from Mexico City, didn't look like much from the outside, but she'd learned that those were the best places to stop. The food was almost always homemade, and there was nothing like the touch of a family working together when it came to cooking a meal.

Tru pulled out his wallet, and she sat up. "No, I commandeered your rental. I can pay for lunch."

"It's really okay. If I weren't here, I'd be at another restaurant paying for a meal." He shot her a half-smile and laid down enough bills to cover their tab.

Just when she thought she'd picked a favorite expression of his, another shot out of the gate. "You have a great smile."

"Not nearly as great as yours."

She stood and held her hand out. "Okay, Mr. Charming, let's go get some cheap knickknacks. Because I love to dust."

He took her hand, but instead of letting it go like she thought he would, he kept their fingers tangled. A gesture she liked and could easily get used to. She wrapped her free arm around his bicep and leaned on him. When had she ever felt so safe? It was more than just his size. There was something about him that drew her to him.

They left the restaurant and strolled to the end of the sidewalk before crossing and making their way back. Inside the shop she'd spotted, there were numerous items with foreign countries stamped on the bottom. It made her rather sad because she was sure there were artists and pieces from nearby talent.

What made the looking so fun was how slow Tru moved. He wasn't in a rush to get in and get out. Most men merely tolerated this sort of thing, but not him. He actually seemed to enjoy it.

"Hey, check this out," he called from the far corner of the store.

When she reached him, she was pleasantly surprised by the local artist showcase. "Why isn't this shop filled with things like these?"

There was an assortment of necklaces, small word workpieces, and a few paintings. There wasn't a lot of it, but at least it was local. She knew most tourists were buying things for their kids or grandkids, but stuff like this told a deeper story.

"My youngest nephew loves tigers." He picked up one of the carvings and then another. "My niece is all things shark. She's eleven, but we have a secret pact. I pass her the stuff inconspicuously, and she maintains her cool street cred." He laughed.

"Do you like having a big family?" she asked as she picked up a necklace.

Nodding, he said, "Yeah, our Christmases are packed, but it's all I've ever known."

She debated a second. "Do you want a lot of kids?"

He snorted. "No. I love my mom, but I'll be good

with two or three." He picked up another carving, looking it over. "I don't want to have kids right away, either." He lifted his gaze to hers. "I want to spend time getting to know my wife, who she is as a person, and enjoying the relationship."

Kayleigh's heart skipped a beat and then hit the speed of sound. He was looking her in the eyes while he said it. Like he was speaking about her. "I feel that way too. About whoever I marry. I think getting to know each other helps keep the relationship solid during the hard times."

"Exactly. No matter how long you know someone before tying the knot, living with them is different. It takes time to adjust and find the rhythm." He smiled.

Goosebumps raced down her back. If they weren't standing in a store, she'd be wrapping her arms around him and kissing him. She'd find another job. A better one with a boss who didn't point out her faults all the time.

After gathering a few more items, they headed to the front and paid. Farther down the sidewalk, there was a clothing store that piqued her interest, and they sauntered that way.

"I like this kind of stuff. Just looking around, checking things out," Tru said as they stopped at a rack set just outside the shop's door. "I think my mom would like that shawl. She has a hundred of them and swears she can't have too many."

Kayleigh bumped him with her shoulder. "Because it's true, and the same goes for blankets."

He laughed. "My mom would—" The sentence died, and he caught her by the elbow, pulling her into the store and putting his back to the road.

"What's wrong?" she asked.

Tru leaned in, whispering, "Those men we picked up the statue from…I just saw one of them." His eyebrows knitted together, and he worked his jaw.

She sucked in a sharp breath. "Here?"

"Yeah. And if there's one, there's more. We have to get out of here."

"Okay. What do we do?"

His gaze swept from one side of the store to the other. "This." Pulling her with him, he plucked a pair of sunglasses, a large sun hat, and a long shawl from a shelf, handing them to her. "Put them on." Then he grabbed a cap, smashed it onto his head, and put on a pair of sunglasses. "You pay. I'm going to get the van. We can switch drivers when we put a few miles between us and these guys."

London would kill her if she found out, but Kayleigh figured it was better for death to be figuratively rather than literally. "Okay." She lifted on her toes and kissed him. "Please be careful."

"I'll keep you safe; I promise."

They walked to the counter, and Tru pulled out a few bills from his wallet. "She'll pick up what's left."

He didn't even wait for a response before peeking out the entrance and then taking off at a run. When he disappeared behind the restaurant where they'd parked the van, her heart was in her throat. What if he got hurt? She'd dragged him into this whole mess. It would be her fault.

It wasn't until she saw the van pull out onto the street that she breathed a sigh of relief. He stopped in front of the shop, looked in the rearview mirror, and then waved for her to get in the van.

The door was barely shut before he took off. It was nothing like all the spy movies she'd seen, which she knew were unrealistic. Why would anyone squeal their tires when they were trying to avoid suspicion?

As she buckled her belt, she slouched in the seat. "Oh my goodness. That was scary. Do you really think they were following us?"

Nodding, he kept his eyes on the road. "Yeah, I do. London needs to be more careful in how she acquires her art."

That's exactly what Kayleigh was thinking too now that she wasn't scared to death. Although, her pulse was humming, and there was no chance of being tired for a while. At least until the adrenaline wore off. "She probably has no idea. Many of the sales she does are with facilitators, and they don't even own them directly sometimes. It's really a mess if you ask me."

When she'd logged all those items, she'd noticed a few odd things. An item would come in, go to a client, get returned, and then sold to another. Sometimes, museums would loan the gallery a piece, and it would go to the appraiser and then get returned. Only sometimes, she'd spotted little anomalies. She'd brought them to London's attention, but she'd just waved it off as inexperience on Kayleigh's part.

"I'm so sorry for ruining your vacation. If I'd just—"

He took her hand, glancing at her. "I'm not. Those men would have hurt you had you been alone. I wouldn't have wanted to live with that."

She wasn't the Queen of England, but if she were, she'd be giving him knighthood status. He really was a once-in-a-lifetime kind of man. While she didn't want to throw everything she'd worked for away, she didn't want to let him get away either.

Squeezing his hand, she said, "It wouldn't have been your fault. I could have told London no, but I agreed to escort it."

"Did it feel like you had a choice?" He pulled his hand free and put it back on the wheel.

"Not really. Most of the time, she phrases things to

make it sound like she's asking me, but the tone conveys something entirely different." London wasn't what Kayleigh would call predictable, personality-wise. Some days she was easy-going and others she was a tyrant. "Although, to be fair, I have made a ton of mistakes. It would be enough to stretch anyone's patience."

She crossed her arms over her chest and touched her thumb to her mouth. "I wonder if we could find out who those men were. I should have thought to take a picture or something. Maybe we could have given it to the police."

"It's a good thought." He chuckled. "Detective."

Wrinkling her nose, she smiled, fanning her fingers out. "I'm shaking. I didn't even realize it until just this moment." She dropped her hands to her lap, setting her forehead against her knees. If Tru hadn't been with her... She stopped the thought in its tracks. He had been there, and she was fine, but the what-if was nipping at her heels.

Sitting up, she shook her hands out. "I think the adrenaline is wearing off."

Tru checked the rearview mirror and then took the next exit. He drove past a few stations to one featuring a car wash. He pulled in and set the brake. "It's okay. They aren't following us. We got away safely. You handled that fantastically. You didn't panic or shut down. You were awesome."

Gentle, sweet, protective...and now comforting. Tru really was the guy a girl waited her whole life for.

Kayleigh unbuckled her seatbelt, slid across the bench seat, and hugged him around the neck. "Thank you."

His arms wrapped around her in a bear hug, like she was something precious to him. "I'm glad I was here."

When the shaking subsided, she leaned back. "Guess we should get back on the road, huh?"

He caught her gaze and held it. It almost seemed like he was at war with himself, but there was no reason for it. She leaned forward to kiss him, but he shook his head. "I want good things for you. I want to support your goals. Let's make it to Houston and then talk, okay?"

She couldn't lie, it stung a little, but at the same time, her respect for him grew. He'd listened to her, unlike any of the guys she'd dated. Tru cared enough to let her fly.

"Okay." She quickly kissed him on the cheek. "And thank you for listening to me."

"Let's change seats so you can get back to driving." He smiled.

As they switched, Kayleigh palmed the spot over

her heart. He'd just fortified his position as the man of her dreams, and she was totally falling for him. They'd talk in Houston, but she knew exactly what direction she wanted to go.

Anywhere he went.

This time she wasn't giving up anything. She was gaining someone to walk through life with.

15

*A*fter leaving the car wash, their run-in with those men had taken up much of their road trip conversation. During the seat switch, Tru had texted Ryder about what happened, and he'd finally agreed that something was off. Those men were supposedly arrested, so how were they following them? There was no way they'd been booked and released that quickly. Until they knew who the leak in the case was, Tru needed to maintain his cover.

Four hours later, once they put in enough miles that Tru was comfortable stopping, they started the hunt for a place to stay the night. They reached a town a little larger than most they'd passed through called San Luis Potosí. Big enough to have more than one hotel and a selection of restaurants while maintaining a quaint feel.

They'd checked in, washed the day off, and found a

little place that pulled them inside by the nose. The food was great, featuring traditional *pozole*, but the company was the star in his opinion. This time they'd shared a single meal and dessert. Tru liked buttoning his pants, and if he kept eating the way he was, he wouldn't make it back to North Carolina with clothes that fit.

"Good food, and I don't hurt." Kayleigh laughed and hugged his arm. "It's nice out tonight, too."

"Yeah, it is." Tru slid his free hand into his pocket. "I do miss the festival, though. That was fun."

She nodded. "Me too. I think it would be fun to make it a yearly trip just to go to that."

As they reached the edge of town, the streetlights grew dim and the twilight sky stretched endlessly. In the distance, the silhouette of mountains finished out the framing, and Tru was positive he'd seen this exact scene in a painting.

"This is beautiful," Kayleigh said. "And relaxing."

"I could certainly sleep out here." Tru tipped his chin to a bench seat a few feet away. "Want to sit for a second?"

"Yeah, we may not have another chance to enjoy something like this."

"Good point."

They strolled to the bench and sat. A comfortable silence stretched between them, and Tru pictured nights just like this one spent with her. Quiet, just the two of them, and the rest of the world forgotten.

"I think I could do this every night." Her soft voice broke the silence.

"Yeah, I could too." In North Carolina, on the Guardian Group property, there was an older cabin that one of the original team members had fixed up a little. When Tru was needing space, he'd stay there to clear his head. The sky was packed with stars at night. He even enjoyed storms there.

Kayleigh snuggled closer, putting her legs over his lap, and sighed. "I don't think I've ever been this comfortable with someone before. Not just because we have things in common. It's more than that."

"I know what you're saying." Exactly what she was saying.

One of the reasons he'd hugged her so tightly while they hid in the car wash was the realization that she could have been hurt or worse. The thought had broken him. It had been less about comforting her and more for his own sake. A world without Kayleigh Kingston would be a dark place. His world would simply crumble to dust. An odd thing to feel when he considered the length of time he'd known her, but that didn't seem to matter anymore.

She lifted her gaze to his. "You do?"

"Yeah." A perfect night, and he'd never had the

desire to kiss anyone as much as he wanted to kiss her right at that moment. He so wanted to, but he knew once she found out they'd met because of his job, it would hurt her. She'd feel used, and he didn't want that.

His resolve to keep his lips to himself was challenged when she brushed her lips against his. He couldn't kiss her. He couldn't. His head screamed that it was wrong, and his heart begged him to give in.

Again, she swept her lips across his, and all the reasons he couldn't kiss her evaporated. Everything—the world around him—faded except her warmth, the way her soft body melded against his, the serenity he felt with her in his arms, chasing the loneliness away.

He wrapped one arm around her, pulling her even closer, and cupped her cheek as he touched his lips to hers. It went beyond the physical for him. Her soul had come along and gently tapped his, breathing life into it. Now, he couldn't fathom his world without her.

Her hands slid up his chest and hooked around his neck as she coaxed his lips to part, deepening the kiss. It quickly went from slow and soft to hard and demanding as he buried his hand in her hair. The longer he kissed her, the more his soul entangled with hers.

Their kisses began to slow again, but they felt entirely different this time. For him, she was it. He knew it defied all logic, but he loved her. It was as true and pure as anything he'd ever felt. It didn't matter if he had an hour or a hundred hours to spend with her, he wanted her, and she was the only soul that would ever fit his.

The thought flooded him with a sadness that crushed him. He broke the kiss and gulped air. "I think we should probably get some sleep so we aren't dragging in the morning."

She trailed light, leisurely kisses from his lips, across his cheek, and down along his jaw. "I'll drink extra coffee."

His head said to make her stop, and his heart begged for more. The war ended when she ran the tip of her tongue across his lips. He took her face in his hands and held her in place as he took command of the kiss this time. Maybe if he put his heart, mind, and soul into it, there would be a chance she'd remember it and know without a doubt that his feelings for her were real.

After kissing Kayleigh until his vision was blurry from the lack of oxygen, they returned to the hotel. Again, he promised himself he wouldn't kiss her and failed. They kissed goodnight, he walked straight to the shower and stood under the cold water until he was freezing.

Now, lying in bed, it was a little after midnight, and

his thoughts were a jumbled mess. Everything from desperately wanting to kiss her again to raging about what he'd do to the guys who could have hurt her. How was it that it had only taken a couple of days for her to upend his world? He'd been feeling lonely long before he took this case, but that didn't explain the pull she had.

His phone began buzzing on the nightstand, and he grabbed it, answering, "Got anything?"

"Yeah, we do." Noah's voice caught him off guard.

"I was expecting Ryder." Tru sat up on the edge of the bed.

Noah took a deep breath. "He thought it would be a good idea if I called with the news."

Great. Most likely, Ryder had told Noah about Tru's resistance in believing Kayleigh was guilty, but he'd wait until the boss brought it up. "I hope it's good. The way those guys were talking…" He let the sentence trail off, unwilling to give the words voice.

"It's not. Those men were to let her leave with the statue, and then they were planning to jump her at the border."

This didn't make any sense. "I thought she put a hit out on them."

"That was what we believed at the time."

Tru stood and walked to the window. "Would you mind hearing me out on something?"

There was a long pause before Noah replied, "Sure."

"I think London Carter is framing Kayleigh." It was the only theory that made sense anymore.

"Okay, why?"

"Well, for starters, Kayleigh had a pretty severe head injury when she was twelve. She was in a coma for a month, and when she woke up, she had to relearn how to walk and talk. I read her file countless times, and I don't remember that being in there."

A rustle of papers sounded in the background. "I don't see that at all. There is nothing indicating any medical issues."

Tru grinned. "London knew that. It was a question on the application Kayleigh filled out."

Noah rifled through the papers a little more. "I'm looking at the application, and that's not on there."

"I know. That's what's got me thinking it's a setup, and when you add that Kayleigh's head injury gave her issues with blackouts and forgetfulness, it changes things." Tru sat in the chair by the window and peeked out, checking the parking lot.

"That doesn't mean she's innocent."

"Maybe not, but over a year ago, Kayleigh had an MRI and was cleared by her doctor. She hadn't had any blackouts or major memory loss until she started at the gallery."

Noah was silent a few moments. "If that's true, then that puts a different spin on things."

"Exactly. NYPD has been trying to catch London Carter for how long? And this mole has thwarted it each time they set up a sting. What would be the best way to fix the whole situation? Carter isn't stupid or she wouldn't be where she is. This feels like a framing job."

Tru continued. "I have another theory too. I don't think London set out to frame Kayleigh specifically. I think the mole told her about the operation and she used the job opening as a way to find someone she could frame. I think she planned this the whole time. Kayleigh was just the golden goose, so to speak. With her head injury and history of blackouts, she was the best candidate."

Noah cleared his throat. "They're respectable theories. We'll need to dig into her medical history to verify it and find out why we didn't see it when we took the case. I think we'll keep it in-house too." He paused, and the distinct noise of his chair could be heard. "It also explains the unsettled feelings I've had about those detectives. I think the mole is one of them, if not both."

"Which would explain why those guys followed us. Kayleigh didn't put a hit out on them; someone put one on her. Again, all roads lead to London Carter."

"All right. I'll take those theories into consideration; however, until we can get a little more information and verify it, you still need to keep your cover."

Tru leaned forward, balancing his elbows on his knees. "I know, and I will. I have a favor to ask too."

"What's that?"

"Kayleigh has a sister named Meesha Kingston. She's returning to the states after teaching in Paris. While she was there, she broke up with a guy, and he wouldn't let her be. We both know that predators typically find a way to get to their prey. Is there any chance we could spare a guy and reach out to her?"

"Wait, sister?"

"Uh, yeah. She's got two." Tru knitted his eyebrows together. "I know. Doesn't match the file."

Noah cursed under his breath. "According to her file, she's an only child."

"Yeah."

"Okay, your theory just jumped to the top of the list. Keep your cover until we can get confirmation. Once we have that, we'll go from there."

They ended the call, and Tru set the phone on the nightstand. He lay back on the bed with one hand under his head and the other resting on his stomach.

It was well-known how Noah met Mia, that a lie had started the entire thing when Noah was under-cover to bring down a sex trafficking ring. In the end,

Mia had forgiven him because there had been a noble reason for all of the deception.

Wasn't this case just as worthy? People were murdered, with one being an innocent man. Didn't his child, a carbon copy of Tru's baby brother, deserve to see the people responsible brought to justice? That boy hadn't lost his dad; the man had been taken. Giving his family closure had to mean something. Tru certainly felt that way.

Maybe when Kayleigh learned the whole story, she'd understand and forgive him. For now, he'd hold on to hope that she would and prepare for the worst.

16

*K*ayleigh had floated lighter than a cloud when she'd returned to her room. That scorching kiss with Tru was the kiss to end all kisses. She'd thought their previous kiss was the standard that all future kisses were to be judged against. Oh, how wrong she'd been.

Then, after he'd walked her to her room, she'd been treated to another one of his blistering, soul-branding kisses that made her dizzy. She'd literally had to pull herself away from him. As far as ever kissing someone else, she was ruined. No one would ever be able to kiss her like him.

Like there would ever be anyone who made her feel the way he did. He was everything she'd always wanted. Of course, she knew he wasn't perfect, that they would have arguments eventually, but she also knew they would be able to work them out.

After belting out a few pillow-stifled squeals, she'd taken a long, hot bath to relax. It had been great for her muscles and soaking away the harrowing flight from that town, but it had done nothing to cool her when it came to Tru. He was hot, his kisses were hot, and he made her tingle all over.

She turned into a raisin before dragging herself out of the tub and getting dressed. Then she made herself as comfortable as possible by grabbing every flimsy pillow she could find and stuffing them behind her back as she lounged in bed. Even with all of them, her shoulders still touched the wall.

Once she was a little calmer, she decided to fire off a text to her sister. About Tru. There was no debate when it came to not telling her about the men who had followed them. There was nothing any of her family could do, and now that it was over, it would only make them worry. She'd gotten away, and she was fine. Because of Tru.

Her ringtone screamed, "You're so fluffy, I'm gonna die," and she put it to her ear, answering Autumn's call. "Hey."

"Serendipitous! It's just so kismet and cute. Oh, I want that."

Kayleigh could picture her sister with hearts in her

eyes and a goofy smile. She rolled her eyes. "You're a doctor. You're supposed to be all clinical and stuff."

"When it comes to surgery and internal organs, I can be cold as a steel bedpan."

"Gross." Kayleigh laughed.

Autumn scoffed. "Love is different. Finding a soul mate can't be quantified. It's mysterious and wonderful and amazing. I love love."

"Tru and I have known each other for two days. I have a job I'm holding on to with white knuckles, at least until I finish this task. You and Meesha are so successful. I know there's no pressure on me from you guys, but I want more." She chewed her lips a second. "I think I'm applying for a different job when I get back to New York. I can keep this one while I find another, but it's time to move on instead of just staying somewhere I'm not happy."

"That's different. You usually just leave."

"I know. It's that new-leaf thing I'm trying out." Plus, she wasn't putting up with London any more than she had to. Tru was right. London treated Kayleigh horribly, and she didn't deserve it. "He lives in Denver, but I'm so torn. I left the last place for a guy, and look how that turned out."

"Kip was a jerk from the get-go. Plus, you were restless. You were talking about leaving Clovis long before you met him."

Now that Autumn mentioned it, she did recall being unsatisfied with where she was. "I'd forgotten about that."

"It's okay. That's why you have me."

Kayleigh took a deep breath. "Autumn, I'm falling for him, and it scares me. I've never felt like this before. We have so much in common. I can see a future with him."

"I can't wait to meet him. What do you think Dad will say?"

"I think they'll love him, but I think that's moving too fast. We have only known each other for a couple of days. When I think about it, I have to wonder if that last MRI was correct."

Autumn huffed. "Just because your jerk of a boss says you have problems doesn't mean you do. You were cleared a year before you started working for her. You were fine. I just don't trust her."

Kayleigh smiled. Her family was so protective of her. "I know, but I can't be sure. I mean, who knows. Maybe the stress of moving to New York, the terrible breakup with Kit, and then working at the gallery set me back. It's possible I *was* at fault."

"I just find it hard to believe. You hadn't had an episode for a year. *A year*. You were fine. I'm telling you, Kayleigh, she's exploiting you."

That was a huge accusation. "But why? What would be the purpose of that?"

"I don't know, but just watch yourself. I don't like London."

"You've never met her. You don't know her."

"I don't have to know her. I know you, and—"

Kayleigh's phone buzzed. With a quick peek at the caller ID, she put the phone back to her ear. "That's London. I have to go. If I don't pick up, she'll just keep calling."

"Okay, be careful. I love you."

"I love you too. I'll call you later."

She switched lines. "Hi, London," she said, keeping her tone light and friendly.

"Kayleigh, are you okay?" The words were rushed and laced with panic, which was unusual for her. Cool and collected was status quo for her.

"Uh, yeah," Kayleigh replied. "I'm at the hotel, I've got the keys to the van, and everything is just fine. Although, those men I met were scary. They were gang members and had guns. They followed me from Mexico City."

After swearing under her breath, London barked a few words to someone Kayleigh could hear in the background and then returned to the call. "Those men were trying to rescue you. That man you're with, he's not just a guy. He's using you."

Those men were trying to rescue her? Then why did they say such nasty things about her? They certainly didn't look like the kind of men who rescued people. They'd looked like the kind to be rescued from.

Her phone dinged. She lowered it from her ear and checked the message.

There, in black and white, were Kayleigh and Tru, eating dinner at the Gran Hotel. It had been amazing and romantic. And fake? Her heart shrank by ten sizes, and her thoughts zeroed in on her time with Tru.

"I just sent you a photo. Is that the man?"

"Yes, his name is Thaddeus Turner." London had to be wrong. Tru wasn't that kind of person. "Where did this photo come from? Is someone following me?"

"A detective showed up just a little while ago, asking about that artifact and you. That's the picture he gave me. He said that man works for a black-market ring. He has ties to some really dangerous people. *He's* killed people. Whatever he's told you, it's all been a lie to gain your trust."

"No. I don't believe that." Couldn't, wouldn't. There was no way Tru was like that. It just wasn't possible.

"I'm putting you on speaker," London replied.

"Hi, Kayleigh, I'm...Detective Smith."

"Tell her what you told me." The acoustics made London's voice sound off.

"Ms. Kingston, we've been tracking the man you're with for a while now. His name is Thaddeus Truman, and he's a ruthless killer. You can't trust anything he says." He paused. "He'll lie, cheat, and steal to get what he wants. He's left a trail of broken hearts and bodies."

Kayleigh's stomach twisted, and she held it. "He's been lying? This whole time?" But he'd rescued her from those men. He'd held her, comforted her, had so many things in common with her…kissed her like she meant the world to him and held on to her like no one ever had before.

"I'm so sorry, Kayleigh. I had no idea." This time when London spoke, she wasn't on speaker.

Kayleigh slid off the bed, walking toward her luggage. If all the things London was saying were true, she needed to get away from him. "I'll get dressed now and leave."

"No," London said. "Stay with him and the artifact."

"But if he's trying to steal it, wouldn't it be better to leave? What if he tries to hurt me?" Not that he could hurt her any more than she already was. All those visions of her future with him, instantly gone. In their place, a hole in her heart and soul that she had no idea how long would take to heal.

"No. Just act normal, like nothing's wrong. He's

resourceful, and stranding him won't work. He'd catch up with you, and there's no telling what he'd do. He's wanted in several states. They said as long as he thinks you're oblivious, you're safe."

Kayleigh's lip trembled as tears washed down her cheeks. Why was she having such a strong response to a man she'd met the morning before? How had she fallen into the trap she always fell for? "So, stay here, with him? How long?"

"I'm working with the detective and the Mexican police." The phone sounded muffled again. "They're wanting the address where you're staying. They'll be there by tomorrow morning. Once he's in custody, I'll arrange to have you fly back. I just feel awful. I'm so sorry." London sniffled. "Just so sorry."

That was the first time London had ever apologized to Kayleigh. Maybe this was why she was so harsh in the past. Getting close to people and caring about them created the chance to have your heart broken. "I'm sorry I've made so many mistakes. I should have listened to you when you told me I shouldn't trust him."

London sighed. "You're kind and trusting, and that's nothing to be sorry for. I wish I wasn't so jaded, but this business is filled with cutthroats and under-handed people. I'm sorry I let that hurt our relationship."

"At least something good came out of this, right?"

"Yes, and I'll try to remember it in the future." She sniffed again, and the sound of yanking a tissue from the box could be heard. "Okay, you get some sleep if you can. Help is on the way, Kayleigh, just be strong."

"Yes, ma'am. Thank you." She ended the call, walked to the bed, and curled into a tight ball. One sob turned into a thousand as the wretched feeling of being used fully settled in around her heart.

How was she going to make it seem like nothing was wrong? Especially when this man made her feel nauseated. Even the idea of hearing his voice was repellent. All the things he'd said...he'd held her, kissed her...

London had told her to get some sleep, but that wasn't possible. As the sun peeked over the horizon the next morning, she dragged herself from the bed to the bathroom. A hot shower wasn't going to fix anything, but if Tru saw her before the police arrived, there would be no way she could play the part of a dupe.

After standing in the shower until she was sure her eyes were no longer puffy, she dressed and returned to the bed. Her eyes had barely closed when a knock came from the door. She pushed off the bed and rushed to it, pulling it open. Not the police.

Tru's eyebrows knitted together. "Are you okay?" He took a step forward.

Instinct and heartache made her flinch away. "I'm fine." The force it took to smile nearly broke her.

For a second, he held her gaze, and it seemed like he didn't know how to respond. "Did you want to grab breakfast somewhere?"

No, because all she'd do was throw it up. She'd aim for him. "Sure, I could use some orange juice."

"Sounds good." He crossed his arms over his chest. "I was thinking we'd get it to go so we can get a little more distance between us and those men. Just in case."

What should she do? The police were supposed to be arriving soon, and London had told her to act like nothing was wrong. She'd just have text London to let her know they were leaving so she could inform the police. If Kayleigh drove the speed limit, maybe they could guess how far ahead she was and catch up to them when they stopped for gas.

"Yeah, that sounds great. You grab your bag, and I'll meet you at the van." She didn't wait for a response; she just turned and let the door close in his face. Probably a wrong move, but until he was in hand-cuffs, passive-aggressive was all she had.

Grabbing the handle to her luggage, she slipped her purse onto her shoulder and hurried to the van. While she waited for him, she sent London a text. Then it hit her. She'd given this man information about her family, but what could she do? If she sent them a message, they'd worry.

The opening of the back door startled her, and she jumped. Clutching her chest, she inhaled and slowly exhaled. "Sorry."

"No, that was my fault. I should have given a warning or something," he said as he shut the door. A second later, he got in and buckled up. "I think I want more than orange juice."

"Sure." She knew it sounded clipped, but how could she be expected to pretend as though her heart wasn't breaking? Tru had used charm to trick her, and the more she thought about it, the angrier she got.

He looked at her with what she would have called concern, but now that she knew the truth, it was just so she'd let her guard down. "Kayleigh, have I done something to upset you? If I have, please tell me."

Drawing on all the strength she had left, she turned to him and smiled. "My bed was horrible last night, and I'm so tired. I'm sorry. Unfortunately, crankiness after a bad night's sleep is a quirk of mine too." It nearly broke her as she looked at him. Even with what she knew, she felt peace and comfort with him. Betrayed by not only him, but her heart.

"I hear you. We all have days." He paused, acted like he was about to say something else, and then waved it off. "I think some coffee and a pastry or two should go a long way in helping."

"You're right. I should put something in my stomach, and maybe the sugar will help." A warning bell went off, and she mentally silenced it. Maybe the stop would slow them down enough for London's people to catch up with them. She wasn't going to let him ruin her trip either. Whatever time she had left there, she was going to enjoy.

He rested his head against the back of the seat. "I have to admit, this whole trip was nothing like I expected it to be, but it's the best one I've ever taken." He rolled his head and smiled. "I especially like the company."

Yeah, right. Jerk. She stuck the key in the ignition and turned it, put the van in reverse, and drove to the exit. There was still no sign of anyone coming to catch this creep.

She could hang on, though. There would be satisfaction in seeing his surprised face when they took him away. For now, that's what she'd use for fuel.

17

*T*ru's talk with Noah hadn't helped in the sleep department. If London Carter had sent those men to hurt Kayleigh, he wasn't taking any chances. He'd kept watch on the parking lot the entire night.

Once the sun began to rise, he'd taken a shower to wake himself up and packed. At the last second, he decided to wear his weapon. He just had a funny feeling, and the last time he'd ignored that, he'd found himself in trouble.

Part of the pep in his step was knowing he'd see Kayleigh. Of course, the worry was still there. She'd returned his kisses with an equal amount of passion and want the night before, but he'd realized it didn't matter how she felt. He loved her. Whether she hated him or not, he couldn't deny what he felt for her.

Something had shifted, though, most notably, her behavior. She said nothing was wrong, but her body language wasn't in agreement. There were dark circles around her eyes, and when he'd looked closer, they were a little red like she'd been crying.

Since hitting the road a little more than an hour ago, she'd been uncharacteristically quiet as well. The bubbly personality he'd come to adore seemed to have a shadow cast over it that extended well outside what would be called her personal space.

The silence was becoming more than he could handle. "I know you said you were cranky, but..." He didn't want to press her or make her feel like she had to talk to him. His words were failing him, and he was running on fumes. "You would tell me if I'd done something wrong, wouldn't you? If I've—"

"You lied to me." She glared at him and then back to the road.

His breath caught. What could he say? "I—" He certainly wasn't going to keep on lying. How had she found out, though? He suspected London, but how did that woman find out?

"Are a liar!"

"Yeah."

She jerked her gaze to his. "No defense? No denying it? Nothing?"

Shaking his head, he closed his eyes. "No." Even if

he gave her answers, she wouldn't believe him, and rightfully so. This was why he hated lying so much. Now he wasn't just dealing with the possibility that those men would catch up with them; he had a woman he needed to protect who no longer trusted him. It was going to make his job harder and more dangerous.

Her lips pinched together, and she took a few deep breaths. "I will not cry over you. I will not! You lied to me. You used me. For what? To steal a statue. And a butt-ugly one at that." She clamped her mouth shut.

"No." His cover was blown, and he knew that would blow up in his face, but stealing? "I didn't want to steal a statue."

"I don't believe you. All you've done is lie. No wonder we have so much in common." She tried swiping a tear away, but it was quickly followed by too many to stop. "You were hoping to catch me off guard and take off with this van."

What? Where was she getting that from? "No, Kayleigh, I don't want that statue. Well, I don't, but it is stolen. Just not by me."

"London and that detective said you'd kill me if you found out I knew, but..." She took a shaky breath. "They told me to act like I didn't know, and I tried, but...the more I've thought about it, the angrier I got. I guess I'd rather die than pretend I don't know."

"What?" He was genuinely perplexed. Kill her?

"The detective said they've been tracking you for years. That you're resourceful. You'll lie, cheat, and steal to get what you want. You've left a trail of broken hearts and bodies in your wake. I guess you can add me to the growing list." She held his gaze long enough that he could see a little anger in her eyes, but most of it was betrayal and hurt.

He shook his head. "I am a Marine. I have killed people, but I have never killed anyone for any other reason than self-defense. There is no trail of broken hearts either, except maybe mine."

"Yeah, right. London said you'd say anything to keep the ruse going."

He had to try to diffuse the situation. "I know you're hurt, and it's completely justified. But think about it. If that were true, why would I have stopped the van to get you yesterday on the way out of town when those men were following us?" He kept his tone soft and neutral.

"I don't know. Probably just because you like being cruel and awful."

"Do you really believe that?" Yes, he'd lied about the reason why they met, but nothing else had been a lie. Somewhere deep inside, she had to know that. He wasn't expecting a miracle, but he *had* hoped they wouldn't end up as enemies.

Kayleigh jerked the van to the right and pulled into

the parking lot of a station they were about to pass, rammed it in park next to a pump, and jumped out. "I believe you lied to me and used me, and nothing you say means anything anymore because you are a horrible, deceitful man without an ounce of compassion or concern."

She pointed her finger at him and leaned in. "You are a worthless, horrible, despicable human being. I trusted you, and you..." Her voice caught. "I..." Her eyes searched his for a brief moment. As her bottom lip began to tremble, tears pooled in her eyes. "I hate you." The van swished from side to side with the force of the door slamming before she took off at a run toward the station.

The words thrown at him were a club, but he wouldn't hold them against her. He'd seen the anguish in her eyes. At the moment, though, he didn't have time to grieve—but he could feel an agony akin to venom spreading, etching through his heart and carving out an abyss he wasn't sure would ever heal.

Pulling out his phone, he tapped Ryder's number. The line picked up, and Tru said, "Kayleigh knows."

"You told her?"

"No, I think London did. The question is, how did she know?" According to the file they'd been given by the NYPD, they suspected one of the people on the team had been leaking information, so only the chief and the two detectives knew about Guardian Group's involvement. Noah's reservations about the detectives seemed more substantiated by the minute.

Ryder let off a stream of curses. "We have a problem, then."

Tru leaned his head to the right and watched the entrance to the store in the passenger-side mirror. Kayleigh might hate him, but that didn't change his need to protect her. "Yeah, we do."

"Are you okay?"

"I'm fine. I knew this was how it would end." Crushed. The only word that fit how he felt.

"Knowing it and feeling it are two entirely different things. I'm sorry."

A trio of cars passed the station, all with black windows and out of place. When they didn't show signs of slowing, Tru split his attention between the mirror and Ryder. "I'll deal. Did Noah tell you my theory about London setting Kayleigh up?"

"Yeah, and, actually, it makes a little more sense."

"How—" The cars drove by again, having turned around, and Tru didn't take his eyes off the road this time, even when they'd passed him. His breath caught when the lead sedan slowed, turning into the station. "I have to go. We have trouble." He didn't even end the call. He just shoved the phone in his pocket, flung the door open, and took off for the station.

"Kayleigh, we need to go," he said as he pounded on the bathroom door.

"I'm not leaving. Go ahead and take the stupid statue. I don't even care." The level of venom in her voice nearly made him take a step back.

He palmed his forehead. How was he going to get her out of there before they were trapped? "If you didn't care, you wouldn't be crying buckets of tears, would you?"

A second passed, and she yanked the door open. The hurt on her face and in her eyes would be a picture seared into his brain for the rest of his life. "Fine—"

Grabbing her by the elbow, he began pulling her to the door. "We need to go."

As tiny as she was, she was fierce. Her hands struck like snakes with pinches and slaps as she tried to get loose. When that didn't work, she chomped down on his hand. Sheesh, she was worse than his mom's anti-social spastic raptor-cat when Tru had rubbed his belly too much.

"Let me go," she said, biting his hand again.

"Ma'am," the woman attendant's voice came from behind Tru. "Is this man bothering you?"

Kayleigh looked him in the eyes. "Yes, he sure is."

Tru turned to the woman. "Sir—" she said.

Tru took Kayleigh's face in his hands, looked her in the eyes, and said, "Kayleigh. Look." He forced her attention to the window. "You see those cars? The men in them are not here just for me."

Shoving him, she twisted free. "Yes, they are. London sent them. They're the police, and they're here to arrest you." A smug smile lifted her lips as she crossed her arms over her chest. "I hope you rot."

The last word was barely out of her mouth when the window shattered, spraying splintered glass everywhere. He quickly wrapped his body around hers, shielding her. Little pieces cut through his shirt and buried into his skin. The second it stopped, he pulled his weapon from his holster, grabbed Kayleigh's hand, and fired before ducking behind a row of chips.

"I said, let go!" If it were possible, she bit him even harder this time, not wasting a second before darting off.

"Don't!" He lunged for her and missed.

Without even a look back, she ran for the door and pushed out of it. "He's right behind me."

Tru smacked into her back as she stopped in front of a man holding a gun. This man was sent to make sure there were no witnesses. At least, that's what Tru's gut screamed.

"That's him. He's the one who was trying to steal my van." She threw a look over her shoulder and back to the man. "Well, aren't you going to arrest him?"

"I'll go willingly," Tru said, holding up his hand. "Just let her get to the van, okay?"

The man flicked his gaze from Tru to Kayleigh and back to Tru. The gunman's eyes narrowed, and the corner of his mouth lifted just a fraction. He went to raise his arm, his free hand coming to the pistol grip as he aimed at Kayleigh. The question wasn't if he going to shoot, but how quickly he was going to pull the trigger.

This time, Tru moved faster than he'd ever moved before, jumping in front of Kayleigh and enveloping her. The world stilled as gunfire rang out, and the smell of sulfur hovered in the air. He felt a pinch as if Kayleigh was fighting him again. "Kayleigh, stop fighting me." Before the next shot, he held her around the waist and dove for a nearby car to shield them. "We have to get to the van."

Wide eyes stared at him. "He was going to shoot me."

The same man yelled a few foul things in Spanish and laughed. When the chorus joined him, Tru's heart sank. How was he going to get her out of there safely when he was so outnumbered? He tried the car door's latch and then looked at Kayleigh. "I know you're hurt and scared, but I need your help."

Slowly, she nodded.

"I'm going to open this car door. I want you to stay

as low as you can and put the gear in neutral. They may start firing, but I won't let anything happen to you. As soon as you switch the gears, I'm going to push this car as close as I can get it to the van, and then we're going to run. Okay?"

Again, all she did was nod. "Uh-huh."

He didn't want to take her choice away, but with as dazed as she was, he couldn't count on her to think clearly. "I'll drive us out of here, and when we're safe, you can have it back."

"Uh-huh."

For their sake, he hoped she wasn't in so much shock that she was just physically reacting. He fired off a shot as he opened the door and then ducked again. Relief flooded him as Kayleigh did exactly as he'd told her. Using his back, he grimaced as the cuts on his back stung and it twinged from putting so much force on getting the car to roll.

A hail of gunfire ripped through the windows, showering the interior of the car with glass. As soon as the car hit the van's front bumper, Tru wrapped his arm around Kayleigh's waist, holding her against his chest as he rushed to the van, shoving her in the driver's side and jumping in. He cranked the engine and threw it in drive. Bullets pelted the vehicle, and he pushed Kayleigh down to the floorboard as the passenger-side window shattered.

"Stay down."

Pressing the pedal harder, Tru didn't bother looking behind him. The very next road he came to, he slowed the vehicle enough to take it before hitting the gas again. The one thing about the route they'd taken was the terrain. Most of it was rocky with a few mountains. If he could find a spot to park where they'd be hidden, it would give him a chance to make sure Kayleigh was okay, and then he could call Ryder.

Luck seemed to shine on him when he came to a grouping of rocks. He checked the mirror and found nothing but open road. Somehow, he'd managed to get far enough ahead that they weren't able to catch up. He eased the van onto the side of the road. Weaving it through the small brush, he finally reached the shelter of the rocks and slowed to a stop.

"I think we lost them." He looked at Kayleigh. "Are you okay?"

Her gaze met his. "That man was going to kill me."

"But he didn't. You were great." With the adrenaline wearing off, he was beginning to feel the wear of outrunning a gang. "You're safe. That's all that matters." That was *all* that mattered.

18

"*Y*ou saved my life," Kayleigh said as she tried to process what happened at the gas station. She'd been so consumed with rage at the store that it hadn't even clicked that the store window was shot out. Her only goal at the time was getting away from Tru and seeing him arrested.

The way that man was dressed: the sunglasses, the tattoos…all of it should have been enough to stop her in her tracks. Instead, she stood there gloating that he was there to get Tru. Then that man had looked at her, pointed his gun, and Tru had wrapped his body around her. It had happened so fast. Way faster than any television shows she'd ever seen.

He smiled, but it lacked his typical energy. "Are you okay?"

She lifted her gaze to his and nodded. "I think so." A dark red stain spreading on his gray t-shirt caught her attention. "But you aren't."

Tru looked down, touched his side, and then looked at his hand. "I need something to stop the bleeding." He lifted his gaze to her. "There's a medical kit in the back."

Taking care not to cut herself from all the glass on the seat, she pulled on the door latch and jumped out. She raced to the back, retrieved the kit, and ran back to the driver's side, pulling the door open.

Her heart sank. The left side of Tru's shirt was soaked. "I said awful things, and you still...protected me?"

"I promised I wouldn't let anyone hurt you." He grimaced as he wrapped his right arm around his middle. "You have every right to distrust me, but I keep my promises."

Kayleigh pulled her gaze from his side and looked at him. "But..." She stopped short. His face was pale, and tiny beads of sweat were breaking out on his forehead. Instead of saying another word, she opened the kit and dug in it for something to stop the bleeding. "There's some bandages and isopropyl alcohol to clean out the wounds."

Tru unbuckled his seatbelt, eased himself out of the seat, and wobbled as he grabbed the door. "I have..."

His voice faltered. "I have some shirts that can be used to clean it."

Rather than respond and waste time, she hurried to the van and pulled out one of her long skirts. By the looks of the wound, he'd need more than just a t-shirt. She returned and pressed the fabric to his wound.

With a grunt, he closed his eyes, and his body went rigid. "I need to sit down."

She scanned the area, and all she saw was dirt and rocks. "Let me grab one of the sleeping bags, okay?"

"Okay." The word was so soft she barely heard it as he pressed his hand against the fabric. "I've got it."

As soon as she was sure he had a solid hold on the skirt, she ran to get the sleeping bag. She flung it out and returned to him. "Lean on me," she said, taking his left arm and stretching it across her shoulders.

If she'd gone one inch farther than the sleeping bag, he wouldn't have made it. His knees buckled, and he cried out as he sat down hard.

"You probably need to lie down," she said, kneeling next to him.

Closing his eyes, he nodded, and she lunged for him as he fell, trying to ease another hard landing.

It was all she could do not to panic. What was really picking at her was how clear her mind was, but she'd visit that later. She leaned back. "I'm going to get the medical kit and some water. I'll be right back."

Nodding, his eyes closed.

As she stood, she pulled out her phone and called Autumn via video chat. The line picked up, and Autumn answered, "Hey, sis. Calling to talk about the cute guy?"

"Yeah, but not the way you're thinking. He's been shot."

"Shot? What? Are you okay? What happened?" The questions came in quick succession.

"Just help me help him, and I'll tell you everything. I've got water and a medical kit."

With that said, Kayleigh's focus turned to Tru's injury and her sister's instruction on how to stop the bleeding. Thankfully, the bullet had gone straight through. Once things settled a bit, she was sure she'd dissolve into a puddle of tears. For now, she needed to keep the man who'd taken a bullet for her from bleeding to death.

After getting him taken care of, she balanced the phone between her shoulder and ear while she took a bottle of water and walked a few paces away. As she washed her hands, she started from the beginning and told her sister everything.

"Do you know who he works for?" Autumn asked.

Kayleigh checked on Tru a second and then walked far enough away that she was sure he couldn't hear her. "No, and I don't believe that detective either."

Somehow, Kayleigh was maintaining her composure. "If he'd left a trail of bodies, he would have added mine to it. Autumn, he could have dumped me at any time and gotten away. Instead, he saved my life. None of it makes any sense."

Her sister lifted an eyebrow. "It makes sense if London was part of it. I'm telling you, something isn't right about her."

"I just—"

"Kayleigh, do you remember what just happened? Are there any missing minutes? That gallery cannot be more stressful than what just happened."

"I froze while we were being shot at." It had been so surreal. One second, she was so spitting mad she wanted to boil Tru in oil, and the next, she couldn't think at all.

"Yeah, anyone with no training would have, and that doesn't mean you're having blackouts or memory loss." Autumn huffed. "Seriously, Kayleigh, that woman is bad news."

"Tru!" a voice called out.

Looking at her sister, Kayleigh shrugged and then peeked around the van. Tru's hand was limp with his phone cradled in it. "Autumn, I'll call you back."

"You better!"

Kayleigh pocketed her phone, walked to Tru, and picked up his phone. "Hello?"

"Kayleigh?" The man spoke her name like it was both a fact and a question at the same time.

"Yes, that's me. Who is this?"

"I'm Ryder Whitlock, and I work with a company named Guardian Group. It's a security team that operates out of North Carolina." He paused a second, and she heard shouts in the background. "Is Tru okay?"

"He's been shot. We stopped at this gas station, and these men attacked us. He passed out after I got the bleeding stopped—or tried to." Her eyes misted over. "He...protected me. They would have killed me." The last word came out strangled.

"Listen, Kayleigh, stay calm, okay? My friend still needs you to focus for right now. Normally, I'd say we'd send a helicopter, but we don't know who to trust right now."

She would've laughed if the situation wasn't so horrible. "I don't know who to trust either."

A Facetime call dinged. Should she answer? What if he was actually the bad guy? Maybe putting a face to the voice would help her discern whether he was telling the truth or not. A man with blond hair smiled. "I'm Ryder Whitlock, and I work for Guardian Group Security Team."

A woman with dark hair quickly took a spot next to him. "I'm Mia Wolf."

"Okay, how do I know you or Guardian Group can be trusted?"

Mia pushed on Ryder's shoulder, and he rolled out of the frame. "I've been where you are, not knowing who to trust or what to do. Nothing but chaos and confusion."

Well, the woman was either a great liar or she really had been in Kayleigh's shoes. "Everything happened so fast."

"Same. One minute I'm standing in my hotel room, and the next, bullets are flying. My choices felt ripped away."

Kayleigh nodded. "Yeah."

Leaning in, Mia's posture softened. "You need to ask yourself a question. If Tru were really the bad guy, would you still be alive?"

Kayleigh's gaze drifted to Tru. London and that detective had made him out to be a monster. Someone willing to do whatever it took to get the job done. He'd had plenty of opportunities to kill her and take the van, but he hadn't.

Instead, he'd saved her life. He had cuts all over his face and on his arms. While she'd tended the gunshot wound, she'd noticed at least two other bullets had grazed him, one on his left bicep and the other on his ear. She looked down at herself, taking stock. She had a few cuts, but they were insignificant in number compared to Tru's.

She brought her gaze back to Mia and shook her head. "No, I don't think so, but he lied to me."

"Yes, he did, but if you help us, maybe we can lessen the sting of that," Mia replied. "Like I said at the beginning, I know what you're going through. Your heart hurts like it's been picked up and wrung out. It's an ache so deep you don't have words to describe it yet."

Well, that was accurate. Her emotions were so mixed up, she wasn't sure she even trusted herself. Despite knowing she'd been lied to, her feelings for Tru hadn't changed. She cared about him. More than cared. While taking care of him, she couldn't stop the word *love* from floating by like a banner. At the same time, her head screamed, *Liar!* "Okay, how do I lessen the sting?"

Ryder rolled back into view. "Tru said you have the gallery's laptop."

"Yes, I have it. What will that do?"

"I think it might help shed light on what's going on, but Mia and I will need it to do it." Ryder picked up a box of Hot Tamales and dumped some in his hand. "I know it's hard to trust us right now, but we are the good guys. Just give us a chance to prove it."

Kayleigh chewed her lip, debating. That laptop was

London's, but... "Okay," Kayleigh said. "If you think it'll help."

"We really do," Mia said.

"What do I need to do?" Kayleigh asked.

She had no idea why she trusted these people when one of them had spent the last three days lying to her, but for some unknown reason, she did. Part of it was Mia and how she described in detail exactly what Kayleigh was feeling.

Looking at Tru, she wasn't sure what she wanted. No, that was a lie. She wanted him to be the hero. Her hero. Chuck without the chafed thumbs. And taller. For now, she'd give Mia and Ryder access to London's laptop and cautiously hope she got the answer she wanted.

19

The scent of alcohol mixed with baked earth drifted under Tru's nose as he opened his eyes. A tiny campfire lamp was the only thing giving him the ability to even make out that the van was still parked. At least Kayleigh didn't hate him enough to leave him stranded. The fact that she'd helped at all gave him a little hope that he might salvage a little of their friendship.

He struggled to roll over and yelped. It had been a bad idea, but he couldn't keep lying on the rock poking him in the back.

"You need to stay still." Kayleigh's face came into view as she leaned over him. "Are you thirsty?"

Cupping her cheek, he brushed his thumb across it. "Are you okay? You weren't hurt, were you?"

"A few matching battle wounds, but I'm fine. Other than shot, how are you feeling?" She smiled.

"I'm—" He balled his right hand into a fist, bracing it on the ground, working to sit up as he held his side with his left hand. With her help, he managed to get upright, although it had taken what little energy he had left. "All right. Been worse." He kept his hand braced on the ground. "We need to get moving. It's dark, and this will be the best time to make tracks."

She set her hands on his shoulders. "Easy. We'll get back on the road in a little bit."

"I'm sorry I lied to you. I didn't—"

She rested her hand on the side of his face, looking him in the eyes. "I hurled awful things at you. I called you things I've never called anyone in my life, and you still wrapped yourself around me to keep me from getting hurt. That bullet was meant for me." She crossed her arms over her chest. "I still don't know how I feel about all the rest, but you did save my life. I *can* be grateful for that."

"You were hurt and angry. With every right to be. I did what I did because it's my job." Of course, it was more than his job. He loved her, but he wasn't going to lay that on her. Not after lying to her for days. "I'm just glad you're okay."

She chewed her bottom lip. "I was...am hurt and

angry. Not at you exclusively, but London and the whole situation."

He tilted his head and knitted his eyebrows together. "Situation?"

"I spoke with Ryder Whitlock and Mia Wolf," she said with a shrug. "I guess you answered the phone and then passed out. It happened while I was talking to my sister after she helped me take care of your wound. I heard someone calling your name and answered it."

"I don't remember. But you talked with them?" If she had, maybe he was able to explain what was happening.

Nodding, she replied, "Not a whole lot, really. They asked me to trust them. I don't know why, but…I did. They wanted access to London's laptop, and I gave it to them."

"You can trust them, but…I doubt me vouching for them gives it any weight." His body was flipping the light switch from on to off. If he didn't get to the van, there was no telling how long they'd be stuck wherever they were.

"I need to get up." He swayed a little as his arm tried to buckle. If he got up now, he could get to the van. They were in the middle of nowhere, and there was no telling what those men would do if they found Kayleigh. With the way they had spoken about her the day she picked up the statue, there was a good chance they wouldn't just shoot her the next time.

"What you need is some water and a little more rest." She left him and returned with a bottle dripping with ice water. She uncapped it and put it to his lips.

Until that moment, he hadn't realized how dry and sticky his mouth was. It seemed to blaze a cool trail all the way to his stomach. He emptied the bottle and gasped for air. "Thank you."

"You're welcome." She chewed her lip. "How did those men even find us? London said she was sending help, but that was before we left the hotel. She didn't know we weren't going up the coast. I kind of forgot to tell her my plans had changed. She told me all this stuff…about you, and I was so upset. I wasn't thinking about anything else."

He knitted his eyebrows as theories developed. "Your phone maybe, but I'm not positive. I checked the van for trackers each morning."

Her jaw dropped. "You did?"

"Habit." He chuckled and grimaced. "No laughing."

"How would she track my phone? Wouldn't I have to give permission?"

He sighed. "I'm sure there are ways around that, but honestly, Ryder is the guy who can answer that question."

Kayleigh gasped. "The laptop."

"That's a definite possibility, but if Ryder and Mia have access to it, it's not tracking us anymore." He shifted a little, trying to take the pressure off the arm he was bracing.

"I knew I didn't take her laptop."

Shaking his head to keep himself awake, he asked, "She said you did?"

"Yeah, I was in the airport bathroom drying my skirt." She paused, and even in the little light they had, he could see the color darken in her cheeks. It was cute she was still embarrassed about that. "She called me. I said I didn't have it, and she made me check my bag. I had no idea how it got there."

A wave of exhaustion hit him, and he closed his eyes. "When you said you had a clear MRI, I knew. I didn't have proof, but it just made more sense then."

This time, his arm buckled, and he didn't have anything left to keep himself upright. He fell back onto the sleeping bag, the force knocking the air from his lungs, making him cough as the water came back up. He could hear Kayleigh, knew she was trying to help, but all he could do was cycle between trying to breathe and handling the excruciating pain. The dimmer clicked off, and the last thing he heard was his name being called.

*T*ru slowly came to, trying to fight grogginess clinging to him. The alcohol he'd smelled earlier had burned off, and now he was left with dirt. It wasn't as dark as before. His entire body was sore—his abdomen and chest most notably, and he was almost positive that if he rolled over, he'd find his lung that he'd coughed up.

"Hey," Kayleigh said, palming his cheek. "You had me a little worried there for a while."

"I worried me too." Breathing too deep garnered sharp pains that shot through his lungs and down into his diaphragm. He grimaced and wrapped his arm around his middle. He closed his eyes again. "I really want some water, but I don't know if I can sit up or trust myself not to choke on it."

A wisp of air swirled around him as he felt her leave and return. "Here, I won't let you drink so fast this time."

With a small nod, he lifted his head as she slipped one hand behind his neck, lifting him enough that he could drink a little. It took a few minutes, but he got enough down that he was okay for a moment.

"Thank you." He took a few shallow breaths. "Give me a minute, and I think I can make it to the van. If I can't, then you need to go without me because I can't protect you. The best I could do is get us both killed."

"I'm not leaving without you." Kayleigh scoffed.

Tru looked at her. "You need to. If Noah hasn't sent a helicopter, there's a good reason. It means he doesn't trust coming across the border. You need to get to Laredo so they can protect you."

She blinked. "What about you?"

All he cared about was her. "You can't stay here. If they figure out where you are..." He cleared his throat, working to keep his emotions in check. "They'll hurt you."

Her eyes locked with his and remained that way as the silence stretched. Little lines creased and smoothed around her mouth and eyebrows again and again as her thoughts played on her features. Never had the urge to read someone's mind hit as hard as right then. Finally, she pulled her gaze from his and vehemently shook her head. "No. I won't do that."

He lay there, summoning every ounce of energy he had left, before he rolled to his right and sat up. A wave of nausea hit the pit of his stomach, and he forced it away as he pushed off the ground. He stayed low to the ground with one knee supporting him.

"Hold on. I need to get the glass off the seat."

Closing his eyes, he nodded. He just needed to keep

himself upright and awake long enough to get in the van. He could do that.

He pushed off the ground and straightened. By his calculations, he had just enough gas to get to the van before his legs gave out on him.

Kayleigh sidled up next to him and drew his arm over her shoulders. When he tried to resist the help, she just gripped his hand tighter. "You are pigheaded."

"And you aren't?" He shot her a smile.

She grumbled something he couldn't quite hear in response and rolled her eyes.

Once he got safely inside the van, she loaded the rest of the camping gear and slipped into the driver's seat, setting the medical kit and several water bottles at his feet, which struck him as smart.

He leaned his head back. His body was shaking from the exertion, and breathing as deeply as he was made everything hurt. If they found trouble on the way to Laredo, which he estimated to be six and a half hours away, he was going to be useless.

As his eyes closed, all he could do was pray that nothing *did* happen, that Mia and Ryder found what they needed, and that it helped ease the hurt he'd caused Kayleigh.

20

*S*ince getting them back on the road, Kayleigh had kept a close eye on Tru. As restless as he was, she would be stopping soon to change his bandages.

Another whimper, this time louder than the others, came from him as he shifted in his seat. Why wasn't he just lying down?

Kayleigh touched his shoulder. "Tru, I don't know how much more comfortable it'll be, but if you want to lie down, you're welcome to try it."

He braced his hand against the dash. "I know you're upset with me. I don't want to invade your space..." His face contorted in pain as he shifted yet again.

This was not the man London and that detective

described. If he was anything like that, he would only be concerned about himself. "It's okay. I'll be fine." She gently tugged on him, encouraging him to take her suggestion. "Come on."

Holding his side, he unbuckled his seatbelt, and the effort it took to stretch out on the bench seat had sweat forming along his hairline. His color was worse too. "Thank you." His voice was weaker as well.

She palmed his forehead, and the heat almost made her withdraw it. "I think you might need a little more water," she said, taking her foot off the gas.

"Don't stop. I can do it." He reached for one of the water bottles and grimaced as the tips of his fingers worked to get the bottle closer. Stretching a little further, he found it just outside his grasp and quit. Just the small amount of energy he'd expended had him breathing hard.

The extra movement of lying down had made changing his bandages a priority that couldn't wait. "I need to change your bandages."

"They can wait."

Kayleigh took her hand from his forehead and palmed his chest. "No, they can't, and you need to stay hydrated." She scanned the road ahead in the little town they'd just entered and found what looked like a boarded-up restaurant. When she reached it, she pulled in, drove around to the back to hide them from the road, and put it in park. She was smart enough to leave it running just in case.

She jumped out of the van, hurried around the front, and got in on Tru's side. Taking the hem of his shirt, she peeled it away and then grabbed the dry shirt she'd stuck in the kit earlier. As she unscrewed the alcohol cap, she said, "Okay, this is going to hurt again."

"I know."

Instead of dousing his wound, she tipped the bottle against the padding of the bandage, getting it as soaked as possible but still keeping the adhesive dry. "Okay, I'm going to do this as quickly as I can."

Nodding, he gulped air and held it.

She pulled back the edge of the bandage and wilted. This was the part she hated most about last time. "All right. Here it comes."

It was just as bad this time, with the veins in his neck bulging as his face turned the darkest shade of red she'd ever seen. She helped him roll to his side and repeated the process. There was no chance it would ever get easier to see him in that much pain.

Once she was finished, she leaned over him and rested her hand against his cheek. The process wiped him out even more, but she had to get him to drink. "Tru."

His eyes cracked open.

"You need water."

Licking his lips, he slowly nodded. There was no help from him at all as she dripped water into his mouth to keep him from hurting himself again. The bottle was nearly dry when he pushed it away. "No more. Thank you."

She hovered over him, and dull eyes locked with hers before fluttering closed. As much as she wanted to hate him, she couldn't. If nothing else, he'd saved her life, and that was worth at least holding on to faith in him a little longer. The all-out agonizing war between her head and her heart was making her miserable.

As she got out of the van, she stopped short as three black cars drove past. She was sure they couldn't see her, but it didn't stop her stomach from hitting the pavement. If these men found her and Tru, she was sure they'd finish the job.

How had those men found them? According to Tru, if the way they'd been tracked was the laptop, Mia and Ryder would have taken care of it. Maybe they had used her phone. The idea of ditching her phone didn't appeal to her, but if that could keep them from continuing to find them, it was worth it.

She hunched down, darted to the door, and grabbed her phone and then Tru's, punching in her sisters' numbers as well as her mom's and dad's. This way, she could at least have their numbers. There was no way she was leaving her phone with all her family and friends on it.

Once she had the phone wiped and reset to factory, she set it behind one of the boards that had come loose.

Hopping into the van, she put it in drive and edged a little forward. Whether it was luck or a higher being, she didn't know, but just up ahead, a van that looked similar to hers was parked at a hardware store.

When the cars parked and the men went inside, she pulled out a little farther, checking the rearview mirror. She wasn't sure if her luck was making up for all the times it had failed her or what, but just a short distance away, a semi turned onto the road, and she quickly darted to the other lane just in time to hide beside it.

She puffed a piece of her hair out of her face and prayed her luck would hold long enough to get to the border.

*S*ince their brief stop and subsequent thwarting of bad guys, Kayleigh had continued to watch Tru. He'd yet to wake up. He was still breathing, although a little too shallow for her liking. It seemed lying down had helped with the restlessness from earlier. Then again, changing his dressing may have had something to do with that too.

As far as how she was feeling now that she'd had a little peace and quiet to think, she didn't know. So far, her emotions spanned a range. Some she didn't even have a real word for. Not quite mad, but if she had a shoe, she'd throw it at him. He'd met her under false pretenses. Had he given her his seat because he wanted to or because he was told to? Pretzels and cheese? His mom? They'd talked about so many things, and now all of them had little question marks popping up.

The worst one of all was the kissing. He'd kissed her, but she remembered seeing the conflict in his eyes. At the time, she was thinking it was because they hadn't known each other very long. Now that she knew the whole thing was a setup, she couldn't help but wonder if that was why he looked so pained.

Her initial reaction to him was that he was kind and gentle, and no matter how much her head argued that it was because he had to be, her heart overruled it.

His phone buzzed on the little ledge sticking out from the instrument cluster, and she answered it. "Hello."

"Hey, it's Mia. How are you doing?"

"Uh, well, to my utter surprise, not horrible." Kayleigh took her right hand off the wheel and laid it on Tru's shoulder. His condition worried her.

Mia chuckled. "That's good because I have some news."

"You found something already?" Not only did she want answers about Tru, but why they'd targeted her in the first place.

"It really wasn't that hard. London might be great at art, but she stinks at computers. Even more so at security for her networks. Using that laptop, we managed to break in and find decades of information." Mia took a deep breath. "And you were absolutely set up."

Kayleigh blinked. "Set up for what?"

"In short? You killed four people and that artifact is stolen. You brokered the deal, and London was unaware of your criminal activities."

"I did what?" Kayleigh squeaked as she shook her head. She had to be hearing things. "What kind of setting up was she doing? I mean, how is that possible?"

Mia snorted. "We only just started digging, so I don't want to say too much until I've got all the information. There *is* a huge paper trail, and everything has her fingerprints. Tru was right. You were being set up."

"Wait, he thought I was set up?" Kayleigh couldn't stop a smile from forming.

Mia cleared her throat. "From the very second he

met you. He called Ryder after you spilled coffee on him and questioned it. He never backed down."

"Really?" She beamed as she looked at him. He'd stuck up for her after... "You mean he told you guys about the coffee?" She groaned. He could have left the embarrassing part out.

Mia giggled. "Yeah, but it's okay. When I met Noah, I ran into a door...and then snorted like Urkel."

Kayleigh snickered. "I don't know. Hot coffee seems worse."

Sighing, Mia's laugher slowly died. "You should know, Tru doesn't like to lie. He's taken some cases like this before and hated it, even with concrete proof they were guilty. I'll let him tell you why he took this one. He's a good man; I promise."

Kayleigh rolled her lips in as tears pooled in her eyes. "Thank you."

"Tru mentioned that you couldn't send in a rescue team. Is there a reason why?"

"Yeah, we don't know who we can trust at the moment, and we don't want anyone being in a situation where it might be an ambush. Tru put a tracking device on the van at the beginning of the trip, so we're monitoring your location and will know when you're getting close to the border."

That actually made sense. "Okay. Tru's really hurt, though. We're just a couple of hours from Laredo, if I don't have to stop and change his bandages again. He'll need medical attention immediately."

"We'll have someone waiting. We'll talk again, okay? And you're free to call me too," Mia said. "I have a feeling we could be really good friends."

What was funny was that Kayleigh had been thinking the same thing. Why, she had no idea, but she did. "I appreciate that."

Kayleigh ended the call and set the phone back on the ledge. That call had given her a lot to chew on. Her boss had set her up to take the fall for four murders. How it was possible was beyond Kayleigh. Didn't that take serious evidence? If so, what had London used?

It also had her questioning all the mistakes London had accused her of making. How many of them were real? The items being logged incorrectly when she was sure she'd put them in right. The lost painting. The laptop? The first time, maybe it had been an accident since they were identical, but this last time? As she went over that evening in her mind again, she tried to —and then it hit her. One of the delivery guys had asked about one of the paintings. Kayleigh had set her bag down on the desk...that hag had switched them. Oh, it infuriated Kayleigh.

Then there was Tru. She quickly glanced at him and the bubbling anger cooled. Her little faith seed had bloomed and poked its head out of the soil. She did...

care about him. The other word was safely locked in a box at the moment until they could really talk. A discussion about how they met needed to take place. Could she trust him from here on out? There wasn't an answer to that yet.

21

"Tru."

He recognized the voice calling his name, but his body was fighting his desire to answer. He was tired and sore. His name was called again, and this time, he forced his eyes open. Kayleigh. She was kneeling next to him on the floorboard of the passenger side.

"Hey," he said. The word came out barely coherent. He cleared his throat and fought the fog a little harder. "Hi."

"You need to drink some water," she said and put the water bottle to his lips. Frosty and cold going all the way down.

She pulled it back a little. "Remember, go slow."

"Where are we?" Now that he had a little more clarity, he realized they weren't moving. Had they made it to the border already?

Kayleigh shook her head. "I had to stop for gas," she said, almost as if she'd read his mind.

As he went to protest, she put her fingers against his mouth. "I parked in back in between two semis. No one can see us from the road. It seemed like the best time to wake you, make you drink something, and check your bandages."

"I'm down for the waking up and the drinking, but that last one is for the birds." He held his side and shifted a little. Both times she'd dressed his wounds, it had sucked his strength and left him breathless.

With a laugh, she let him drink some more. "Well, you weren't so pigheaded this time, and I already changed them. You were out cold. They seem to be holding just fine at the moment. Maybe by the next time you wake up, you'll be in a hospital."

She gave him another good mouthful of water and said, "I spoke to Mia."

"You did?" His heart picked up speed. It was good they were talking. Maybe Mia was able to give Kayleigh the answers she'd need to deal with being lied to and to get her name cleared.

"Yeah, it seems London *was* setting me up. There's more, but Mia wanted to wait until they had all the information. It gave me a chance to tell her how you are, too. She said they are tracking us with the device you put on the van."

Closing his eyes, he smiled. "I knew it. I knew you couldn't be guilty. Even covered in coffee, I was smart enough to know that." Plus, his gut hadn't let him down. She was innocent, and he was beyond grateful.

"She said the same thing. That you never believed it."

"Things just didn't add up. You'd never flown before. I knew that when I lost feeling in my arm." He opened his eyes and looked at her, smiling. "You were just too cute, and there was something about you."

Kayleigh held his gaze. "I was told you don't like to lie. With a name like Tru, I have to wonder why you do lie so much."

"I don't want to. I hate it, but sometimes I don't have a choice." It had been a pillar of his since he was a kid, and it had stayed with him as an adult. One of the worst things someone could do was lie. Trust was too hard to gain and too easy to lose.

"Can you tell me why you took this case?" she asked, scooting a little closer. "Mia said I should hear it from you."

Tru took a long drag of air and let it out as he nodded. "I told you I have a big family, four brothers and two sisters. Only three of my brothers are alive. My mom was running errands with my baby brother while the rest of us were in school. That day, there was a bank robbery, and things went south. My little brother was killed in the crossfire. We never got justice for him. The robbers escaped and were never found."

She covered his hand with hers. "That's...awful. I'm so sorry."

"One of the witnesses in this case, who I'm guessing London murdered but pinned on you, had a little boy. He looks exactly like my baby brother. I mean spitting image. We—my mom—never got justice. It took us kids years to come to terms with it, and we had both of our parents to help. There are still times I'll find my mom grieving. I guess we all do in our own way." He took a deep breath, stopping right as started to hurt.

"That little boy has his grandparents, and that's great, but I want them to be able to tell him that the person who took his dad is in jail. When I saw his picture, it felt like I was supposed to take the case. I guess, in a way, I was trying to give my family the justice we wanted."

"So, not saving the world, but definitely righting it for him." She chewed her thumb.

"What?"

Kayleigh tucked her hair behind her ear and nodded. "I wanted you to have a good reason for lying to me. That's a pretty decent reason."

"I'm sorry." He swallowed hard and rubbed his face with his left hand. "I didn't want to."

"I know." She cast her gaze down. "Give me a little time to digest it all. I'm not saying we can't be friends, but…"

He covered her hand with his, closing his eyes. "It's okay. I broke your trust. You don't have to explain anything to me."

The next thing he knew, she was touching her lips to his cheek. "And when you do things like that, it helps build it back." She smiled and then gasped. "We need to go."

"What?" He'd been a little sleepy just a second before, but he was wide awake now. "Why?"

She lifted up a bit, crawled across the passenger floorboard to the driver's side, and peeked over the dash. "Those men keep finding us. I don't know how. I ditched my phone. You said Mia and Ryder would take care of the laptop, and you've been checking the van. Could the tracking device be in the statue?"

"That's a good possibility too."

"The last time they caught up to us, it seemed like they didn't have an exact location. Like, they were given a broad area of where we were. They got close, but I lost them."

"Last time? What last time?" he asked.

"I'll tell you as soon as I put distance between us

and them." She put the van in gear and took off slowly, checking both ways before increasing the speed. When she hit the highway, she craned her neck and looked in the rearview mirror.

Tru grabbed the back of the seat and pulled himself up. "They're behind us."

"Great," she said and grumbled. "I wish I had a bigger van. I'd run them over."

He grunted as he kneeled in the seat and then climbed over.

"What are you doing?" she asked, jerking her head around to look at him.

"Being useful." He bent low as he walked to the back of the van and pulled up the spare tire cover. If Tru was right, there were a few items that could help them slow the guys following them. Sure enough, he found a bag full of tire spikes. "I'm going to open the back of the van."

Before she could argue, he pulled the back door latch and dumped the spikes. The first car tried to slow, but it was too late, and all four tires blew. The car behind it slammed into the back of the first, and the third swerved to avoid the other two, careening off the road and running into the *Come Again* sign.

With the three cars taken out, he yanked the back door to shut it. It was the green light Kayleigh needed because the second it was shut, she hit the gas.

He took a deep breath and held his side. When he pulled his hand away, he realized he needed something bigger than the bandages he currently had. If Kayleigh saw it, she'd stop again, and they couldn't afford it. There was also the chance that more guys would be sent after them, which meant they needed to keep trucking.

After grabbing the duct tape, he dug in his luggage and pulled out a shirt. He folded it, held it against his side, and wrapped the tape around it until he was sure it would stay.

With that done, he hunched down and climbed over to take his seat again. The shirt stemmed the bleeding, but it did nothing to help the pain or the exertion.

"What did you do?" she asked as she looked at him.

"Just reinforcing the bandages." He wrapped his right arm around his middle. "This way we don't have to stop again."

Her eyebrows knitted together. "I guess. What did you do back there?"

"Tire spikes."

"Oh." She paused. "Where did you get them?"

"Guardian Group put all those extra things in the van before I picked it up. At the time, I couldn't tell you that." He wiped his mouth with his left hand and bent forward to snag a water bottle. "I'm sorry."

"Yeah," she said softly. "Me too."

He needed a subject change. "So, about last time?"

"I stopped in a little town a while ago. After I changed your bandages, I spotted them, but there was a van just like this one parked at a hardware store. I used a semi to drive past without them seeing us, and let's just say I've been creative with the speed limit." She chuckled.

"Based on what I just witnessed, you handled yourself well both times." He stuck the water bottle between his knees and patted himself down, looking for his phone.

"Here." Kayleigh grabbed it off the ledge of the instrument panel and handed it to him. "It has a few of my phone numbers in it because I wiped mine before leaving it in that last town."

He twisted a little to look at her. "You know you're pretty incredible, right?"

Her cheeks turned that perfect color of red that made him want to press kisses all over them. "No, I'm not."

"Yeah, you are." He smiled. "Most people wouldn't have thought of leaving their phone, let alone wiping it. Then you kept an awareness of the area around you. That's...impressive." He laughed.

Kayleigh cut a glance at him, but the smile on her lips was bigger than any he'd seen yet. "You're just saying that 'cause you're broken and don't want to be stranded."

Shaking his head, he relaxed a little more. "I'm not wrong." He touched her arm. "Don't stop again until you get to the border. I don't care what you think I might need. If they happen to send more men after us, they'll send an army." He uncapped the water and took a long drink before sending a text to Ryder about the men. If anyone could figure out how they were finding Kayleigh, it would be him. "Promise me you won't stop again."

For a fraction of a second, he thought she'd argue, and then she replied, "Okay."

He finished off the water and laid his head back, closing his eyes. "Thank you." He just needed their luck to hold out a little longer. Once they were into Texas, they'd be in the clear.

$\mathcal{K}$ ayleigh stole a glance at Tru, and his reason for taking the case played through her head again. His answer hadn't been what she was expecting. Really, it was a plain, simple reason. He wanted justice for a little boy who'd lost his father. Even if that little boy hadn't looked like his baby brother, it was equally solid...and sweet.

Knowing that made it difficult to remain angry with him. She was still upset by it, but he wasn't being heartless. How was she to know any of what they shared was real? His kisses? The ones before London called sure had felt real. It had been blissful. He'd left her with bruised lips and an insatiable desire to keep him as close as humanly possible. He was her one. Learning he'd lied...it had been agony thinking that all of it was to use her.

She also knew he wasn't being completely honest about how much pain he was in. He wasn't okay. He'd taped his shirt around his middle and given her a lame reason as to why. His pale face and nearly white lips completely contradicted what he was telling her. He didn't want her worrying or getting hurt. In her mind, that put him in the realm of noble.

They would have made it to Laredo a little more than an hour ago, but when she'd stopped to take care of him the last time, just before those men caught up with them, it had taken longer than she'd let on. She'd changed his bandages, and he didn't even flinch. It had scared her, and she'd been too afraid to leave his side. Staying still had helped some, and she was finally able to get him to wake up.

She'd also failed to mention that she used cash and bought a burner phone. Mostly because she didn't want him to worry. If London had framed her, Kayleigh reasoned that she shouldn't let on that she knew. It seemed the best way to keep her boss in the dark and keep in contact.

The phone vibrated, and she grinned. She'd purposefully kept the ringer off in case Tru fell asleep again. There was also a little excitement that she felt like she was staring in her own cloak-and-dagger show.

Answering the phone, she said, "Hello?" keeping her voice low.

"Kayleigh, oh, thank goodness! I have been calling and calling." If Kayleigh didn't know her boss was framing her, the concern in London's voice would have been touching.

"I'm sorry. I did what you asked and stayed with the van. We stopped to get gas, and these men started shooting at us. I didn't know what to do, so while Tru was distracted, I got in the van and took off. I've never been so scared in my life. The next thing I know, I'm waking up in the van at a truck stop nearly halfway back to Mexico City." She added a breathy, tear-filled sniffle at the end to make it more believable.

"I'm just glad you're okay. I've been so worried. Where are you now?"

Another question Kayleigh had prepared for while she watched over Tru. "I decided to go up the coast. I thought maybe if I changed my route, they couldn't find me."

London heaved a sigh of relief, or that's what Kayleigh would have thought before she'd been shot at. Her boss's voice was muffled a moment, and she returned. "I'm getting a plane ready so I can meet you in Houston. I don't want you dealing with this all the way back to New York."

"Oh. You can't meet me in McAllen? Don't they

have a big enough airport?" The answer was yes, yes, they did, because Kayleigh had checked. She was a lot smarter than London gave her credit for, but it was smarter to play dumb at the moment.

Her boss faltered a minute. "I wish I could, but a client is offering his plane, and the farthest he's willing to let me take it is Houston."

Okay, so yeah, that was a reasonable excuse, but that didn't mean it was true. "Okay. I will get there as quickly as I can."

"Just make sure you call me so I know you're okay. I'm just heartsick that all this is happening."

Yeah right. Heartsick? Kayleigh would sooner believe jackalopes were real. "I'll call you when I stop for the night to let you know."

"Thank you. Please be safe."

"I will," Kayleigh replied with her sweetest, most innocent voice and then rolled her eyes as she ended the call. She grumbled to herself. The old cow had set her up to be charged for murder.

"Don't think I didn't hear that," Tru said.

Kayleigh squeaked and jumped, palming the spot over her heart as she swerved a little. "What is the matter with you! I could have killed us both!" Her heart pounded against her ribs. She'd been feeling a little tired before the call with London, but with Tru nearly scaring the life out of her, she was wide awake now.

He slowly opened his eyes as he laughed. "You've got a pretty good handle on things if you ask me. What you just did was brilliant. Not saying she won't call your bluff about the direction or figure it out, but that was some clever thinking, getting that burner phone."

The compliment sent a giddy, girlish tickle down her spine. He'd said she was incredible, and he'd looked so proud of her when she'd told him about wiping her phone. "It was just stuff I saw on TV."

"But you applied it to real life. Kayleigh, I was trained to do what I do. You're just…amazing."

She laughed. "You can thank old reruns of *Scarecrow and Mrs. King*."

He rolled his head and looked out the passenger window. "We should be close to Laredo."

"We're about twenty minutes away. We'll have to go through customs at the crossing, but I have all the paperwork in my bag. It shouldn't take long." At least, that was her understanding before she left for Mexico City. What were the chances that London had done something to keep Kayleigh detained? "That's if London told me the truth."

He chuckled. "That's the million-dollar question."

Kaleigh stole a glance at him. Warning bells went

off, telling her she needed to keep him awake. "So, tell me about Guardian Group. How did it start?"

"A woman name Pamela Williams formed it. She lost her husband in a drive-by shooting, and after his death, she learned he'd managed to grow their savings into a fortune. She wanted to honor his memory."

Talk about a way to start a company. "That's both heartbreaking and completely romantic. How did you find them?"

He gave a soft grunt as he shifted in the seat. "After leaving the Marines, I bounced from job to job with security firms because I didn't like my bosses. I didn't like how they treated the people under their protection. My boss, Noah Wolf, approached me about seven months ago and asked if I'd be interested in working for him."

"I guess he must have impressed you."

"At first? Not really because I'd heard the same talk from my other bosses. I knew Guardian Group was different when I accepted my first assignment. This woman figured out that the man she was with wasn't who he said he was. Instead of coming up with a plan and keeping her out of the loop, Noah told her everything. That's when I knew Guardian Group was different."

"How so? Wouldn't telling her make her scared?"

Tru nodded. "Sure, it scared her, but it was better to

be scared in Noah's office rather than somewhere else. Somewhere we may not have been able to control. We can only protect a person so much. They have to be able to participate in their protection. The first person the attacker will try to take out is their bodyguard.

"Plus, keeping information from the people we protect puts them in danger. If they don't know why we're doing things the way we are, they're more likely to fight us. It's a lot easier when the person is willing to work with us."

Well, that information sucked some of the romance out of her favorite shows, but it made sense. "I guess I hadn't thought about it like that. If I'd known what was going on yesterday, I wouldn't have fought you about it and gotten you shot." Guilt hit her all over again.

"It's okay," he said, smiling. "That's why it's better to tell the truth. This case was different than a protection detail. We were going after a killer."

Yeah, her. Only, at the time, they didn't know she was being framed. She couldn't put the entire fiasco solely on their shoulders. The question about the last few days, whether anything was authentic or not, bounced around her brain again.

"Tru, was any of it real?" She'd held on to it until now because she wasn't sure if she wanted to know the answer or if it would matter. He'd lied. Noble or not, what they had was started on a pretense. She wasn't sure how she was supposed to move past that. "I just…"

"All of it was except my last name. I love pretzels, trying new foods, and traveling."

"The…the kissing?" She stole another glance.

"Especially that." He inhaled deeply and let it out slowly. "My feelings were genuine. You are beautiful and funny. Clever and interesting. I've never enjoyed the company of a woman ever in my life as much as I've enjoyed spending time with you."

Silence hung between them until it was almost uncomfortable before he spoke again. "I also know that you feel betrayed, angry, and used. It's okay to feel those things. I know nothing can come of this. I broke it before it started when I lied. I can't take it back or change it." He paused. "If all I get is friendship, which is what I deserve, I'll call that a win."

Nodding, she said, "Yeah, I need to think about it."

"I know," he said just above a whisper.

How should she respond? She didn't want to give him false hope. She also didn't want him to think there would never be a chance. Until she had her feet on solid ground, the future was suspended. Maybe once they were safe and she was sure he would be okay, they could talk again.

Maybe. Big, big maybe.

23

$\mathcal{T}$ru had rested his eyes after answering Kayleigh's questions. The ones about Guardian Group were easy. The ones about him had cut, and they shouldn't have. He'd known that's how she'd feel once she found out. It was a natural response to what she'd been through. If one thing was a lie, then all of it was a lie.

The difference between knowing it and feeling it created a chasm so wide he would have never been prepared for it. He could have fortified his heart with platinum-reinforced rebar and a vault worthy of Fort Knox, and it wouldn't have made a difference. The gunshot he was dealing with wasn't nearly as painful as the heartache.

As the van slowed, he forced the thoughts away and breathed a sigh of relief. If he was right, they'd reached the crossing bridge. To be sure, he opened his eyes long enough for confirmation. Sure enough, they had, and he'd never been so happy to see border patrol in his life. It also meant he was closer to getting Kayleigh to safety.

Ten minutes later, the van slowed to a stop. The agent on duty swept his gaze over the van, and as he walked a little closer, his hand went to rest on his service weapon strapped to his belt. With his free hand, he pulled out a flashlight and shined it on them. It was clear from his body language that he was suspicious. "Passport and declarations."

"I have paperwork in my luggage for a museum artifact that I'm taking to New York." She laughed nervously. "I should have stopped before I got here and gotten that out for you."

Even if the papers London sent with Kayleigh were legit, there was a good chance they wouldn't have let it through unless Noah brought them in on the case. As it stood, border agents were supposed to let them pass through to the American side with an agreement that the statue would be returned as soon as the case was closed.

Tru lifted his head. "Mine's in the back too."

The officer looked a little closer. "Sir, what is that you have around your waist?"

Oh man, he'd forgotten all about that. No wonder

the officer was looking at him funny. He probably looked like he had a bomb strapped to him.

"Uh," Tru said and looked down. "A shirt. My name is Thaddeus Truman. My employer, Guardian Group, should be waiting for me." He sure hoped they were.

The man pulled his walkie-talkie from his waist and stepped away while keeping his flashlight pointed in the van.

Kayleigh leaned over. "They're here?"

"After those men attacked, they should be. I've worked for them long enough that I can make pretty solid educated guesses on their next moves." His lips quirked up.

The officer returned with his hand covering the sidearm he had strapped to his waist. "Sir, I'm going to need you to step out of the vehicle."

"Actually, he's not feeling so great," Kayleigh said. "I have all the paperwork you should need in the back. I work for Beacon Art Gallery in New York City. I'm escorting an authenticated piece of art from the Palace of the Plumed Butterfly."

"Ma'am, he needs to get out of the—"

Tru touched her shoulder. "It's okay. He's doing his job. Everything will be fine."

"Wait!" a voice called out from his walkie-talkie. "We have visual confirmation."

The agent replied, "Yes, sir."

The woman on the other end of the walkie-talkie continued, "Tell them to follow the signs and their party will be waiting for them."

The man looked once more in the van and waved them forward. "Have a safe trip."

The second the back end of the van was safely on US soil, the tension in Tru's neck and shoulders eased and allowed him to relax. Whatever it was keeping him even remotely alert the last few hours faded as the edges of his vision blurred until darkness claimed him.

24

First class and now a private plane configured for a security company, complete with a decked-out emergency room with a television in the corner. If Kayleigh ever had to fly again, there'd be nothing but disappointment waiting for her. Between that and calling London to keep her from getting suspicious, they were the only two things occupying her mind and keeping her from hyperventilating.

She and Tru had barely crossed the border when Tru slumped over. She'd punched the gas and skidded to a stop as men poured out of the door of the border patrol office: Ryder, Noah, Hendrix Wells, and Kolby Rutherford.

While they swept Tru away, they'd taken Kayleigh, all the luggage, and the statue and moved them to another vehicle. When she'd asked about the van, they assured her it would be taken care of.

Mostly, she just wanted to know if Tru was okay. He'd been so pale. She'd known he was lying about the gunshot when he taped that stupid shirt around his waist.

The last time she'd seen him was over an hour ago, and with every minute that ticked by, her worry meter kicked up a notch. What if he'd lost too much blood? But all she could do was sit right outside the room and wait.

"You look exactly like I felt when Noah was shot," Mia said, taking a seat across from her.

Giving her a weak smile, Kayleigh asked, "Was it this bad?"

Mia's gaze flicked to Noah who was sitting near the front of the plane talking with his men. "Yeah, we didn't know he'd been shot. He was lying in the back of the SUV, bleeding to death, when I found him." She sat back, crossed her arms over her chest, and looked Kayleigh in the eyes. "Just moments before that, I'd been so angry with him. As noble as the cause was, he'd lied to me. Worse, he'd kissed me while believing I'd be forced into witness protection."

Kayleigh's jaw dropped open. "Really?"

"Completely serious. I'm not a violent person, but I could have stabbed him with a rusty fork. I had fallen so hard for him, and there he was, telling me that there had never even been a chance for us to be together." Mia rolled her eyes. "Oh, I was boiling mad."

At least Tru hadn't done that. "London told me not to let on that I knew, but I couldn't. I don't think I've ever been that angry in my life. I called him things I've never called anyone."

"Trust me, I totally get it."

"Now, I'm not angry as much as I am confused." Kayleigh's knee bounced as she looked down. "I care... deeply for him."

"Here's the thing you need to seriously consider. These men aren't like most men. What they do is dangerous. Every time they go out the door, there's a chance they'll never walk back in."

Lifting her gaze to Mia's, Kayleigh chewed her lip. "What made you take the risk?"

Mia's face lit up. "Everything is a risk. You can love someone whose job is as normal as can be and still lose them. In my case, I loved a man willing to put his life on the line to help people. I figured if any man deserved to be loved, it was him. And I wanted to be loved by him."

"I've known Tru just a few days."

Holding up her hand, Mia snorted. "I've got no room to talk. I knew Noah a week, and we were married just a few months later. We now have two kids, and we're talking about a third. I wouldn't trade my life with him for all the safety in the world."

Okay, a week was still longer than a few days, but not that long. "Well, that makes me feel a little better." Kayleigh groaned and rubbed her face. "I think the craziest part is...I'm just not all that angry anymore. At first, yeah, but he had a good reason. I just question how much of it was real."

"I did too, and that's something only you can figure out."

"How did you do it?"

Mia's smile went all the way to her eyes. "He didn't have to kiss me. Once I put that with his character, it was easy. He was a good man, and if he hadn't had any feelings for me, he never would have kissed me."

"Good point." She held Mia's gaze. "How did you manage to start working with your husband?"

She shrugged and leaned forward. "I was better with computers than Ryder."

"You were not! Are not!" Ryder yelled from the front of the plane, startling his dog, Rufus.

Mia covered her mouth as her shoulders bounced. "I love messing with him."

Rufus's ears perked up, and he trotted over to Kayleigh, nudging her hand.

"Well, you're a little demanding, huh?" She laughed and scratched him behind the ear.

"He looks like a dog, barks like a dog, has breath like a dog, but I'm not convinced he is one. He's not your average pooch." Mia leaned over and ran her hand over Rufus's head.

The dog looked at Mia, and to Kayleigh, and it seemed like he was telling them he wasn't.

"I have to admit, it's awesome you wound up working with him. I almost wish I was better at computers." Shrugging, Kayleigh sighed. "It would be nice to be a part of something bigger than myself."

Mia grinned. "Who says you can't?"

Kayleigh's eyebrows rose to her hairline. "Because I don't really have a talent to add."

"Sure you do. What we're doing right now is needed. Being a friend to someone when their world is splintering."

Huh, she'd never even considered that, and now that she was, it opened up a whole new world of possibilities. "I guess I hadn't thought about it like that."

Just then, the door opened, and Jax stepped out, another member of the team. Whew, he was cute. Dark, wavy hair, dark eyes, and dimples.

"Bleeding stopped, all the glass has been removed, and he's stable," he said and nearly wilted into the seat next to Mia. The slight country twang only made him cuter. Not Tru-cute, but good-looking. For someone else. "You did good keeping the wounds clean and free of infection."

"My sister Autumn helped me. She's in her last year of residency." Kayleigh smiled.

"He's resting, but if you want, you can go in there with him."

Steeling herself, she stood and walked to the door before pausing. "Thank you…both of you."

As she shut the door behind her, her gaze landed on Tru. Even as beat-up as he was, he looked more fantastic right then than he had the first day she met him. Mostly because he was alive.

They'd treated the bullet grazes. A few places where the glass had made deeper cuts had stitches in them, and they'd wrapped his midsection with gauze. She'd somewhat prepared herself, but there was no way to do it fully.

He'd kept her safe, and if he'd been the kind of man London claimed he was, he would have let Kayleigh die and saved himself. Which meant he wasn't the kind of man to lead someone on.

He didn't have to share his meals with her or dance with her. He didn't have to hold her hand. He certainly didn't have to kiss her, which he was exceptional at. But he'd done all those things.

She sat beside him and leaned over, bracing her hand on the bed. With her free hand, she combed her fingers through his hair and pressed a kiss on his cheek. It didn't matter how they met; she loved him. She couldn't picture ever loving anyone else like she loved him.

They had a few things to work out, for sure, but if he committed to her like he committed to Guardian Group, she had hope that they could fix anything.

---

*T*hey'd reached Houston during the middle of the night and transferred everyone to a safe house Guardian Group used from time to time. It had given Kayleigh the chance to shower—the first time she'd stood still since Tru got shot. She'd come unraveled, had a good cry, and stepped out feeling like a huge weight had lifted off her chest. After, she'd dressed and had a bite to eat, then she'd crashed. Apparently, she'd been running on empty and her body was over it.

She woke up late in the day, called London, and then spent most of her day splitting her time between watching over Tru and talking to Mia. They were still being a little tight-lipped about London, but Mia reassured her that as soon as they had everything, they'd tell her.

After her last conversation with Mia, she returned

to Tru's room and carefully lay down next to his right side with her arm across his chest. It wasn't until she had her arm around him that it hit her how things could have turned out dramatically different. She could have lost him. The idea took her breath away, and she couldn't hold him tightly enough.

Tru stirred, and his eyes slowly opened, his lips lifting in a weak smile. "Hey. Are you okay?"

"I am now." She nearly cried. "You have no idea how glad I am that you're awake."

"It's okay. I'm fine."

She slid her hand up his chest and palmed the side of his face. "You scared me. It took over an hour to get you stable."

"But I'm fine now. And you're safe." The smile faltered. "If you don't want to stay anymore, you don't have to. Don't worry about me. I'll be good to go in no time."

She caught his gaze and held it. "Do you want me to leave?"

With a tiny shake of his head, his eyebrows knitted together. "No, I just don't want you to feel like you have to be here."

She combed her fingers through his hair. "I'm here because I want to be, and I'm not going anywhere unless you make me."

As their eyes remained locked, he caressed her

cheek with the back of his hand. "If that's the case, you won't be leaving anytime soon."

"Then I guess I'll be staying awhile." She smiled, covering his hand with hers. "Let me get you some water, and then you can rest a little more." Standing, Kayleigh walked to the door and paused. "I'll be right back."

Outside, she leaned against the wall and sent up a silent prayer of thanks to whoever might be listening. Now that he'd finally woken up, she could breathe easier. They'd talk later when she wasn't an emotional wreck and he was more coherent.

25

Two days later, Tru almost felt normal for having been shot. He was still grounded to the bed, but he couldn't complain too much. Kayleigh hovered, but he wasn't going to lie and say he didn't enjoy it. Actually, he loved having her near and holding her, even if it was one-armed since it hurt to use both.

They hadn't *talked* yet. He'd come to late the night before, and she'd mentioned something that almost made it seem he'd been awake before that. He was too afraid to press it, though. It felt like he was in a bubble of fantasy, and he didn't want to pop it. He'd already decided he wasn't going to tell her how he felt. They'd been through too much in the last week, and he didn't want to push himself on her. There was also the fact that he'd saved her life. He didn't want her affection because she felt she owed him somehow.

"What are you doing sitting up?" Kayleigh asked. "You're supposed to be taking it easy."

Tru looked over to the door, and there she stood, arms crossed over her chest, looking as beautiful as ever. "I am. All I'm doing is sitting."

She crossed the small distance and stopped in front of him. "I just don't want you reinjuring yourself."

He looked up at her. "I'm not. I was careful."

For just a fraction of a second, she held his gaze, and he couldn't for the life of him decipher what was going through her mind. She walked to the door, shut it, and said, "We need to talk."

His heart went from steady to staccato in a single beat. He didn't want to talk. He was too afraid of what the results would be.

She returned to him, taking the same spot as before. "I've been waiting until I thought you were feeling better, and maybe a little stronger, but I can't put this off any longer."

His heart dropped to the floor. He thought he'd braced himself for the inevitable, but he could've had a century and still would've been unprepared to lose her.

"I've had some time to process everything and think. I was so angry when London told me your real name. So much so, that I didn't even question anything about those men she'd supposedly sent to rescue me. I'd just talked to my sister, and you were the topic of conversation. I knew I cared about you, but I hadn't realized how much at the time. Then I found out you'd lied."

He hung his head, waiting for the blow.

"I had never been so enraged in my life. I thought my heart was literally being ripped from my chest."

"I know," he whispered. "I—"

"I'd fallen in love with you."

Tru jerked his gaze up and grimaced. Apparently, *everything* was connected to the neck bone.

She stepped closer. "Did you hurt yourself?"

"A little, but what did you say?" He couldn't have heard her correctly. Maybe he was daydreaming or something. Or maybe he was dead and just hadn't figure it out yet. He was half tempted to look around for *Beetlejuice*.

Her lips slowly curved into a smile. "I said I love you."

"But…I lied." He'd been positive there was no way forward with her. "I mean, I didn't want to, but I did."

"I've talked a lot with Mia. Seems the two of us share a similar scenario. Which is part of the reason I'm telling you. If you decide to do something stupid like Noah did—and you better not," she said, and her eyes narrowed, "I wanted you to know how I feel." Her shoulders rounded as her gaze lowered to the floor. "I know it sounds absurd, but I do. I love you."

"You…you do?"

A chuckle popped out. "With all my heart. We may have met under a less-than-ideal situation, but I've been wishing for a guy like you for longer than I can remember. It just so happened that the universe answered me, and I can't begrudge the delivery method when I got exactly what I wanted."

Pushing off the bed, Tru grunted as he stood. "I think you deserve someone worthier, but I sincerely doubt they'd love you better," he said, slipping his right arm around her waist and pulling her closer. "Nothing was fake. I held your hand because I felt warm for the first time in my life. I danced with you because I loved seeing you smile and hearing your laughter. I kissed you because there was no way words could describe how much I loved you. I would have kissed you more, but we couldn't sit on that bench forever." He set his forehead against hers. "I love you with everything in me."

"We have a whole lot in common." She lifted on her toes and touched her lips to his.

The delicate kisses were sweeter than the last, and he could picture them growing even more so. The soft, languid way she kissed him in return only made him aware of how hungry he was for her.

He slid his hand up her back and into her hair, holding her still as he left her lips, tasting her skin as he trailed kisses across her cheeks. A soft moan poured from her lips, fueling an even deeper want. He continued the light kisses along her jaw, down the side of her neck, and pressing his lips against the back of her ear.

So caught up, he went to lift her so he had better access to her soft skin, and a shock of pain forced him to break away. He grunted, trying to hold in the pain of the poor choice.

"I'm sorry," he said and eased himself onto the side of the bed, gripping it and breathing through the intensity of it.

"You really do need to rest."

Tru reached for her, tugging her closer, and rested his forehead against her stomach. "This is all I need." The ache subsided, and he lifted his head. "And kissing you was totally worth it." He smiled.

She held his gaze and caressed the sides of his face with the back of her fingers before stretching them into his hair and bending down to kiss him. Just like the last, the kisses were slow and nearly torturous as she touched her lips to his cheeks and forehead, each time bringing her lips back to his and letting them hover just out of reach.

When he couldn't take it a second longer, he

cupped the back of her head, pinning her and deepening the kiss. Her arms wrapped around his neck as she carefully molded her body to his. It seemed she was drinking him in as much as he was her.

A soft knock came from the door, and she sagged against him, groaning. "I'm not ready to stop kissing you."

"It's Noah," said a voice on the other side of the door. "If you want to be a part of the planning, you need to meet me in the conference room."

"Uh," Tru said, and his thoughts scattered with the nuzzle of her nose along his neck, punctuated by light kisses. "Uh...we'll be right there."

"All right, but we're not waiting for you."

Kayleigh leaned back. "Let's go catch a bad guy." She kissed him. "And just so we're clear, I plan to make up for all the kisses I missed."

Why did she have to say that? Tru groaned and reluctantly stood. "I plan to collect."

She grinned and spun on her heels with him following her out the door. When they reached the conference room, Noah, Ryder, Mia, and Jax were already there. Rufus wasn't too far from Ryder, stretched out snoring. Kolby had done his part and returned home.

Noah looked up from his position at the front of the table. "Good timing."

Mia tapped a few keys on her laptop and said, "Tru's suspicion was right on. It was a setup before London Carter posted the job. The department was setting up an operation, and the mole—or I should say moles as it was both detectives—had alerted London to it. Knowing that, she'd used the employment search to find a patsy she could frame before leaving the country."

Tru held his side as he sat forward. "Do the detectives know we've figured out they're working with her?"

"I don't know, and until I'm sure the chief isn't in on it as well, we're not sharing information," Noah said, turning to Kayleigh. "All of that bogus information in the file was being fed to us by the two detectives. That's why we didn't know about your head injury or your sisters. One of the detectives put pressure on a guy from a previous case, a black hat."

"Wow."

Noah nodded. "If Tru hadn't forced the issue, I don't know if we'd have ever figured it out."

"The guy was good," Ryder said, glancing at Mia. "But we're better."

Kayleigh's jaw dropped. "So, all this time…"

"Everything was one giant lie," Noah finished. "From how you were hired, to the hit you put on those men who were there with the statue. All of it."

"A hit? What hit?"

Ryder grunted. "Yeah, that black hat was feeding us that. We'd tapped your phone, or so we thought."

"London gave me my phone before I left. She didn't think mine would work too well." Kayleigh blinked. "This is all a bit overwhelming."

Nodding, Noah looked at Mia. "I think all of us have a taste of what that's like."

"It did help us beef up our system. If someone tries that again, we'll know it," Mia said. "I just wish we'd figured it out sooner. I'm sorry."

Shrugging, Kayleigh sighed. "It's okay. If it helps in the future, at least something good is coming out of it."

As Mia began to brief them again, Ryder passed around photos taken of the area.

Hendrix walked in holding a large can of tea. "Sorry about that. I'm ready when y'all are."

"That story about blacking out and being almost halfway back to Mexico City was good thinking." Noah looked up from the notes spread out in front of him. "We're grateful for the extra time. Did you tell her you were meeting her tomorrow night?"

"Yep, just like you instructed me to." Kayleigh beamed.

"Good job."

Ryder looked up from his laptop. "This client who

loaned her the plane has done business with her frequently, and he has ties to a few unsavory groups."

Hendrix nodded and leaned forward. "When the plane arrived yesterday, I was already in position. I can confirm that I saw several well-armed men were on board. From what I could see, they were taking orders from London Carter. Both of the detectives were there as well. It backs up what Ryder discovered on that laptop. By the looks of it, one of them did something he shouldn't have done. One of the men who arrived with London cold-cocked him, dragged him to a car, and left with him. I call Houston PD, described the individuals and the vehicle, the license plate number, and the possible direction of the vehicle."

Noah flipped through the folder. "Six men?"

"Yes, sir," Hendrix replied.

Leaning back, Noah crossed his arms over his chest. "I don't want to spook her, and I don't want a firefight."

"London still thinks I'm meeting her at the airport with the statue," Kayleigh said. "If I go—"

"Absolutely not." Tru didn't even want her to finish that statement. "No way."

Noah laughed. "Surprise."

Kayleigh looked at Tru. "It's the easiest way. I've played the unwitting employee pretty well."

Shaking his head, Tru replied, "And from the way it sounds, she hasn't bought that at all."

Hendrix sat back in his seat and set his ankle over his knee. "And we can plan for it. You said yourself, Kayleigh is sharp and resourceful."

"She is..." Tru could hear himself walking into a statement that could get him in the doghouse and stopped. "Kayleigh is both of those things, but it's an airport. It's not contained. Even with local law enforcement backing us up, we'll have no idea if London is prepared for the double-cross or not. She's obviously got connections, or we wouldn't have had a gang trying to kill us. There are too many variables, and we can't possibly plan for all of them."

Kayleigh touched his arm. "I think I have a say in this, and I want to do it. She tried to frame me. If anyone deserves to be a part of this, it's me."

He shook his head. "She's killed four people. I don't want you to be number five."

"I don't want to be either, but she set me up. Made me think I was losing my mind. All the little details she said I messed up on, the painting she said I lost, all of it." Kayleigh's lips pinched together. "I have the right to confront her. I want to make her regret it."

"And I get that..."

Kayleigh set her hand on his arm. "I know the risks, and I have the right to take them if I want. I'm not asking permission. You want justice? Well, so do I. I'm helping."

"What you're asking…" Their eyes locked. He was seeing his future with her flash before his eyes. And he desperately wanted that future. If something happened to her, he'd never forgive himself. "I get to ride in the back of the van."

Her jaw dropped. "No way! You're hurt."

"And you're untrained. We go together or not at all."

Noah held up his finger. "Uh, I think that's my call." He gave Tru a pointed look.

Mia bumped him with her shoulder. "And you'll let him do it because you'd be doing the same thing."

Noah looked at his wife. "That's not necessarily true."

She leveled her eyes at him and crossed her arms over her chest. "Really?"

Ryder cackled and high-fived Mia. "I love you."

"Both of you are…" Noah stopped short when one of Mia's eyebrows lifted to her hairline. He cleared his throat. "Back to the subject at hand."

Jax picked up the pictures Hendrix had taken. "Hendrix can take that roof, and I can take the other. We can give cover."

"All right." Noah nodded.

Mia looked at the laptop sitting on the table in front of her. "And I've got eyes."

"Who's flying the drone?" asked Tru.

Noah smiled. "New guy I'm considering hiring. We'll see how it goes." He gave the group one more glance and stood. "All right. Hendrix, you and Jax, get back to that airport and keep eyes on London and crew."

"Yes, sir," they said and stood. "I'm driving," Jax said.

"I don't think so," Hendrix replied.

Jax grumbled, "You drive like a rookie mutton buster. I'm not riding in a car that you're driving."

The argument continued until both men were out of earshot and the front door closed.

Kayleigh barked with laughter. "Are they always like that?"

"Since the day they met," Tru replied.

With Jax and Hendrix off to the airport, the meeting returned to Kayleigh and Tru. His stomach soured at the thought that she would be going into a situation with six armed men, but he also understood the need Kayleigh had to confront London. The woman had nearly wrecked Kayleigh's life. She wanted justice, and he understood that.

Kayleigh's impenetrable courage held strong until she saw London. She was outfitted with a mic so Noah and his team could hear everything. Tru was in the back of the van inside a storage compartment that a crew of welders had added the day before. They'd given Tru enough room to be comfortable and then closed him in with a false back. None of it did anything to ease the urge to throw up.

Men with large rifles were standing around the plane while London was in her typical pose: arms crossed over her chest, head held high, and a look of disdain that seemed to be permanently etched on her features.

Taking a deep breath, Kayleigh parked the van far enough from the plane that it wouldn't be in the way and close enough that it wasn't a hike. She got out and smoothed down her shirt. Noah and the team had done a great job of making her look the part of a distraught, scared woman who'd slept in a van for a few days. Her clothes were ripped and dirty, and they'd even gone so far as to make her hair look disheveled.

About halfway to the plane, London ran to greet her and hugged Kayleigh. She leaned back. "I am so glad to see you."

If there weren't men poised to kill her in a heartbeat, Kayleigh would have dropped to the tarmac and cackled like a wild goose with its feathers ruffled. "I'm so glad to be somewhere I finally feel safe." She sighed.

London took her by the shoulders and held her away, looking Kayleigh over. "You poor thing. I thought you were staying in hotels."

Kayleigh forced a few tears, and her lips trembled. "I was too afraid, and I didn't want to give anyone a chance to steal the statue."

"I should never have been so harsh with you."

Shrugging, Kayleigh hugged herself, resisting the growing urge to sucker punch her. "It's okay. You've been under a lot of stress, and I haven't made things easy."

"Hey, boss, we got a stowaway over here," one of the men called out.

Kayleigh whipped around and froze. The compartment they'd made looked like it was factory. At least, to her it had. How had they even known to look for him?

The man had Tru pinned against the van and a small handgun set flush against his neck. "Seems he's not in top form either." The man switched hands with the gun and poked Tru right where he'd been shot, digging in deeper until Tru cried out and gurgled as the man leaned hard on Tru's throat.

"Stop!" Kayleigh screamed and faced London. "Please make him stop."

London leveled her eyes at Kayleigh and then struck out like a snake, grabbing her shirt and ripping the mic off. She put it to her mouth. "If you don't want them both to die, you'll let me leave with the statue and my treacherous ex-employee. I'll set her free as soon as I get somewhere where I know I'm safe."

She dropped the mic and crushed it with her shoe.

Two shots fired from two different directions, and the men with London ducked down, searching for where the shots could have come from. One man stepped out from the cover of the plane's wings and fired off several rounds.

"You thought you were so clever, lying to me. Acting like you were just some frazzled little idiot, but I knew. I knew the minute I spoke to you that night on the phone about your traveling companion."

Kayleigh glanced over her shoulder at Tru. "He's hurt. Please just let him go. He's in no shape to fight anyone." She returned her attention to London. "That night on the phone, I had no idea who he was. I'd just met him the day before, and he was kind to me."

"Right, and that explains why he was hiding in the van? Is the statue even in there?" London rolled her eyes. "Doesn't matter. I don't need it."

"You only hired me so you could set me up, didn't you?"

"The police were getting too close, and I knew they were close to finding out who the mole was. You were the golden goose, so to speak. Head trauma, blackouts, moments of forgetfulness." She smiled.

Kayleigh stared her down. "Did you get that, Noah?"

London stepped back like she'd been slapped. Her lips contorted, and before Kayleigh could move, the woman pulled out a handgun and jerked Kayleigh into a chokehold. Cold steel seeped through Kayleigh's shirt as London jabbed the gun into her back. "I'm walking out of here. I don't really care if she's alive or dead when I do."

Like a scene unfolding in a movie, whistles of gunfire broke out. Shouts and cries sounded around them. The man holding Tru dropped to the ground, holding his arm. Once the gunfire ceased, Tru pushed off the van and closed most of the distance between himself and Kayleigh before London aimed the gun at him.

"I will not hesitate to kill both of you. All I want is to walk out of here."

Tru winked at Kayleigh.

Just like Tru had instructed and Mia had demonstrated, in one swift motion, Kayleigh grabbed London's arm, biting down on it hard enough that the gun fell from her hand. She used the heel of her foot to kick her in the shin and drag her heel down the length of it before wheeling around and connecting her fist to the side of London's jaw. The woman went down in a heap, groaning as she held her jaw.

Setting her hands on her hips, Kayleigh leaned over and said, "That's what you get for messing with me. The punch in the jaw was for hurting Tru. Unlike you, I'm kind enough not to stomp you while you're down."

Sirens blasted as police moved in, and Kayleigh ran to Tru. "Are you okay?"

He held his side. "I'm okay. I may need a few stitches replaced, but I'm okay. Are you okay?"

She grinned and clapped like a performing seal. "This was the best date *ever*! I kicked her rear. Did you see that?"

Nodding, Tru grinned. "I saw it. You were bad to the bone."

"That was the most fun I've ever had." She wasn't kidding either. It was better than a rollercoaster. She was scared at first, but then her mind settled, and, *wham*, she was ready to kick tail. "Is this how you feel when you take down a bad guy?"

"Maybe not as excited, but it does feel good." He put his arm around her shoulders.

"We'd make a great team, you know." She kissed him.

"Why don't we give our statements to the police and then go discuss it over a big honkin' plate of pretzels?"

She turned to him, held his face, and kissed him. "I love you, Thaddeus Truman. I never thought I'd be grateful for being framed, but I'd do it a million times if it meant I got you."

"I love you. You were worth every last stitch."

EPILOGUE

One year later...

Tru twirled Kayleigh and curled his arm around her as her body floated back to his. They'd returned to the festival they'd only had a taste of the year before. They'd spent their weeklong honeymoon at the same hotel, soaking up the music and culture the event offered.

At least, that was the story they'd given the hotel since they were undercover as newlyweds. Tru had loved the idea of a second honeymoon. He didn't have to pretend he was just as much in love with Kayleigh as when he first met her. He loved her more with every day that passed.

London had been arrested, and she was still awaiting trial. All her bank accounts had been seized, along with the gallery and art, and her choices for legal counsel had dwindled to public defenders.

The men who'd followed them had also been taken into custody, and they were still waiting for extradition back to Africa. The detectives had gotten them out of jail the first time, but it wouldn't happen a second time. London had hired the gang members, and if Tru hadn't been with Kayleigh, she would have never made it out of Mexico.

The NYPD police chief had been cleared, and once all the evidence began to come to light, the two detectives were looking at serious prison time. One of them turned on the other after he'd learned his partner was going to pin it all on him. And in an effort to keep himself out of prison, the owner of the plane London borrowed had given the police all of the flight records and offered to testify against her.

The night they took London down had changed their lives in ways Tru had never predicted. He wanted a life with her, but he'd never expected Noah to be on board with them as a team. With Mia's help, Kayleigh had convinced him it was the best idea in the world. They could travel around, stake things out, find their target, and when the lifting got too heavy, the big guns could be sent in.

It had been sold as a win-win for the entire team, and Tru couldn't argue with the results. They'd already managed to bag four different thieves. Men and women who preyed on the elderly and lonely. It wasn't the same as guns blazing and fireworks, but they delivered justice to people, and that was satisfying. Which was their reason for being in Mexico City once again.

Tru picked her up by the waist, and her head fell back as she laughed, sliding down his body until she was eye to eye with him and he kissed her nose.

She hugged him around the neck, kissing the side of his face. "This has been so much fun."

"Only because I'm with you." Tru planted another kiss on her nose.

She set her forehead against his. "Don't look, but he's sitting right behind you."

"You sure?"

Her eyebrow slowly went up. "Positive. It's not like he's hard to pick out. He's dressed like a peacock." She kissed him. "I have no idea how he's conned so many women out of their fortunes."

"Love can blind a person." Tru laughed.

"Especially with that suit."

He squeezed her. "I guess it's time to work, huh?"

Kissing him again, she grinned. "Guardian paid for this Mexico City *honeymoon*. I don't feel like we can complain."

Tru groaned. "Fine, but I get another dance when we lock this old bird up."

"You bet, Mr. Tru."

"Let's catch a bad guy, Mrs. Tru."

When he'd seen his future with her, this wasn't what he'd planned, but he loved it and he loved her. That was all that mattered to him.

For a list of all books by Bree Livingston, please visit her website at www.breelivingston.com.

ABOUT THE AUTHOR

Bree Livingston lives in the West Texas Panhandle with her husband, children, and cats. She'd have a dog, but they took a vote and the cats won. Not in numbers, but attitude. They wouldn't even debate. They just leveled their little beady eyes at her and that was all it took for her to nix getting a dog. Her hobbies include...nothing because she writes all the time.

She loves carbs, but the love ends there. No, that's not true. The love usually winds up on her hips which is why she loves writing romance. The love in the pages of her books are sweet and clean, and they definitely don't add pounds when you step on the scale. Unless of course, you're actually holding a Kindle while you're weighing. Put the Kindle down and try again. Also, the cookie because that could be the problem too. She knows from experience.

Join her mailing list to be the first to find out publishing news, contests, and more by going to her website at https://www.breelivingston.com.

Printed in Great Britain
by Amazon